JESSE

THE HUNTER SERIES BOOK 3

KATHI S. BARTON

World Castle Publishing, LLC
Pensacola, Florida
Copyright © Kathi S. Barton 2013
Print ISBN: 9781939865403
E-Book ISBN: 9781939865410
First Edition World Castle Publishing, LLC, May 10, 2013
http://www.worldcastlepublishing.com
Licensing Notes
Cover: Karen Fuller
Editor: Brieanna Robertson

Chapter 1

Joey could smell the smoke as she sat down on her makeshift bed. It wasn't strong yet, but she knew that it wasn't because someone was having a fire in their home, nor was it a barbeque grill smell. She tried to ignore it over the exhaustion she was feeling, but she knew that if she tried to sleep now, it wouldn't be happening. Instead of rolling into her bed, she got up and dressed.

"I swear if this is simply a trash can on fire again, I'm going to move to another building." Laughing to herself, she knew that was an empty threat. There were no other buildings, empty or otherwise, where she was. Stepping out into the chilly November morning, she shivered. Soon, she promised herself. Soon she'd have a real apartment.

She walked to the closest building to the one she was in. It, too, was empty of people, and almost all of the furniture and equipment had been removed. There didn't seem to be any smell coming from this one. *Of course not*, she said to herself. *That would simply be too easy.*

She didn't know what had happened to these places but was grateful that she had a place to stay until she could save up enough money to get another apartment. It had been almost eleven months since she'd been tossed out of her other one, and she wasn't going to spend any more time in the cold if she didn't have to.

Just before Halloween last year, they'd all been served. No one had had a clue that the building had been sold, though she was pretty sure the maintenance man had. He'd moved out the month before, and no one had come to replace him or the broken down things in the apartments. Then the letters had come.

Hunter Corporation had sent the letters. It said that they all had thirty days to remove themselves from the property, and they were not getting any extensions. They had been given the previously required ninety days four months ago and, basically, enough was enough. No one she'd talked to had received any kind of notice ninety days or otherwise.

She moved to the third empty building as she thought of trying to get in touch with the person who had signed the letters. J. M. Hunter, Attorney at law, was about as nice as the letter they'd gotten and just as elusive. Even going down to the massive, overly priced building hadn't gotten them anywhere. She had been "helped" out of the building the thirty-first day after she'd been warned without any contact with a single Hunter.

She was just coming out of the fifth building when she saw the smoke. It was billowing out of the second floor, and, as she stood there trying to decide what to do, several of the windows burst out. She was ready to sprint to the nearest payphone when she heard the screams. Damn it all to hell and back. Of course, the place wouldn't be empty.

She noticed the nice cars in front as she ran to the building. She had no idea what they were, not caring a fig for cars anyway. But she did recognize that they didn't belong in her neck of the woods. She broke the window over the back door of the building to get in when she saw the flames coming out of the windows now. The glass breaking was covered by the sound of a small explosion if one could call it that, and she knew she was running out of time. Hurrying into the burning building, she was hit by a blast of heat so hot it took her breath away.

Joey had been in this building once before. When she'd been looking for a place to flop until she could save her money. Not getting a deposit back had hurt all of them, and then when the utility company had told them that their bills hadn't been paid in months, something that had been part of the rent, they'd had to fork over that as well. While she was familiar with the building, she still had to think about where the stairs were.

Another explosion rocked her nearly off her feet as she topped the stairs. She could see flames at one end of the hall and just knew that's where the screams were coming from. She started toward the opposite end when she had to turn back. Someone started yelling again. She found them in the room nearest the fire.

"She's dead. You have to get me out of here."

Joey looked at the well dressed woman on the floor and then back at the one standing in front of her.

"She died of a heart attack, and I'm willing to testify to that fact."

Joey raised a brow at the woman and moved to the one on the floor. Checking her pulse confirmed what Joey could see. The woman was very much alive. She turned back to the other woman. "She's fine, and I can get you both out if you'll help me carry her." The woman was already shaking her head. "You won't help me, then we all die in here. Up to you, lady. I don't really care."

The woman on the floor grabbed her arm as she stood. Joey looked down at her and could see that she was in pain. She hunkered down to see what she was saying when she heard the other woman speak.

"She was going to leave you, Annamarie. This girl was going to leave you to burn."

Joey ignored her and checked on the wound that was bleeding on who she assumed was Annamarie's forehead. "You have a nasty bump here, and if you can walk, it won't be accompanied by some pretty nasty burns." The woman nodded and groaned. "Yeah, I'd try not to do that again if I was you. And for the record, I wasn't going to leave you."

She got Annamarie up without much help from either woman. Joey was just starting out the door when another explosion — this one felt right under them — rocked them all off their feet. Joey had tried not to land on the hurt woman, but it had taken her off guard, and she'd fallen hard. The woman was out again.

Working faster now, knowing that they were running out of time, she got the woman up. She wasn't very big and, lucky for her, Joey was strong. She was moving toward the stairs when she noticed the woman who'd been a shit and not helped was headed for the elevator.

"Won't work. In case you hadn't noticed, there is a fire going on here. Even if there was electricity in this building, you'd be better off using the stairs and not getting in an oven like that if necessary." Joey was on the third step when the woman stomped around her.

"I'm getting the hell out of here. You two can burn the hell up for all I care. No commission check is worth getting my suit all smelly for." Joey watched her go down the stairs, thinking there were all kinds in the world.

The stairs were catching on fire. Most of the top behind them was hot when she'd moved over them, and, when she'd had to lean against the wall to rest a couple of times, she'd felt the rumble of it starting to go. When the woman she had hanging over her shoulders started to move, Joey stopped and spoke to her.

"If you can walk, lady, we might make it. There are at least two dozen more stairs to go and then the walk across the foyer. I'm getting sort of tuckered out."

"I can help. I'm dizzy, but the alternative is not so good." She moved her around to her right side so that she could use the wall as support. With her weight, though slight, gone, Joey could move her along a little faster. "Where is Sondra, the woman who I was here with? You didn't kill her off, did you?"

Joey wasn't sure if the woman was trying to make a joke or had heard her threaten the woman once or twice when Joey had been trying to get her up off the floor. She wanted to be pissy at her about how she was saving her ass, but bit her lip and didn't comment on that.

"She decided that I was moving too slow for her, and she left on her own. I hope she was able to find the door. It's pretty smoky down here." And the lobby was full of smoke.

Annamarie laughed then groaned again. "I fell when the first bomb when off. I know it was something in the basement, but it felt very bomblike. I hit my head, and I'm sure I have a couple broken ribs. Did you know you were bleeding?"

Joey had felt the glass dig into her arm but had been so worried about getting in and out of the building she'd forgotten about it. She knew it was deep too, and painful now that she'd pointed it out.

The lobby floor looked like it was eighty miles wide. Joey had to more or less carry Annamarie across it, but before they were halfway across, another explosion tore through the floor and flames erupted nearly on top of them.

This time Joey remembered to let go of the woman when she was thrown across the room. Lucky for Annamarie, Joey got most of it. She crawled back to the again unconscious woman and had to blink several times before she could see the door. She was in pain now and wasn't sure she'd make it. Grabbing the woman by the legs, she mostly dragged her out. She could just hear the sirens as she got her to the sidewalk.

And Sondra was nowhere in sight. Looking back at the building, Joey saw her. She was in the lobby near the window, waving her arms and looked to be saying something. Joey just knew she was going to regret it and started to rise to go and save the stupid woman. Annamarie grabbed her arm.

"Where?" She closed her eyes again, and Joey thought she'd passed out, but the grip on her arm tightened when she tried to leave again. "Where is Sondra?"

"I have to go and get her. She's near the door, can you see her?" Joey pointed and looked back at Annamarie to see that she had either passed out or was simply resting. Standing, without resistance this time, she went to the building.

~~~

Annamarie hurt. She heard the fire trucks coming but wanted her family too. She wasn't sure she could see the numbers but pulled out her cell phone glad that, since leaving the building, she now had a signal. She pushed a button, hoping she wasn't calling for a hair appointment, though she was sure she could use one and sighed when someone answered.

"Kasey honey, is Royce around?" She loved her new daughter-in-law but was afraid she'd come to her aid with her son. The woman could fight one-handed if the need arose.

"He's in the den with Jesse. Want to speak to him?"

She told her that she did. Annamarie was afraid she'd passed out again when she heard her son speak. Not able to hold on to her terror and what might have beens, she starting sobbing and telling him that she was injured.

"Where are you, Mom? I'm coming right now. I...tell me you're going to be alright."

"Yes," she told him in a watery voice. "I can see the firemen now. I'm at the empty building on Westmoor. The one we've been thinking of buying." She was babbling. "Oh wait, I see...what is she doing?"

She watched her real-estate agent come out of the building with a large piece of wood. When she looked over at her, Sondra dropped the wood and took off running in the opposite direction. Before she could yell at her, the fireman blocked her view. By the time she got him out of the way, she was gone, and Royce was screaming at her.

"The nice fireman is going to see to me. I can see medical personnel very near. I want you to meet me at the hospital. I'm better than alright. I'm going to live." She closed the phone and looked up at the masked man in front of her. "There's a woman in there. I think she's just inside the doors. You have to save her. She carried me out of the building when I couldn't move. Hurry."

He nodded once and moved toward the building, barking orders to several men to come with him. Before they were ten feet from the burning building, the girl came out, staggered out really, and fell. Annamarie watched in horror as the men scooped her up in their arms and ran for safety. The building was coming down in a ball of flames, and, just as the heat started to touch her, someone threw something over her, and she was out again.

Chapter 2

Joey woke with a start. There was a stranger standing over her, and she jerked back before she realized that she shouldn't do that. He chuckled slightly, and she realized how many curse words she'd spewed in a matter of seconds. He leaned back and looked down at her.

"I'm doctor Fletcher Eton. You're at County General. Do you remember what happened to bring you here?"

She watched his face. He didn't seem to be pissed, but he didn't know she was uninsured yet.

"Miss?"

"Fire." Her throat detonated in pain. There was no other way to explain it. And with the pain came why it hurt.

"You have been bruised very badly at your throat. It looks like someone tried to strangle you." He leaned down again and gently touched her. "I would ask you to tell me what happened, but you should try not to talk for at least a few days."

He finished examining her, and she thought about how she had been nearly strangled. That woman Sondra had grabbed her from behind as soon as she'd entered the building. If she hadn't been so exhausted, Joey might have been able to throw

13

her off, but she'd worked all night and carried a woman out of a burning building. By the time the doctor left after telling her that she was going to be admitted, Joey knew it was time to leave. She was just sitting up and waiting for the waves of dizziness to leave when a man walked in.

"Hello. How are you?"

She didn't answer him but did look up. He was probably in the wrong room anyway. Men like him didn't come to see how women like her were. Unless, of course, he was serving her with something like a summons or some other legal paper she couldn't afford. She knew he was a lawyer of some sort.

Tossing back the covers, she was glad to see they hadn't cut off her jeans. A girl was broke these days, and having your pants cut up didn't help. She was holding onto the bed, having gotten out of the bed slowly when he sat in the only chair in the room. He was smiling at her, and she wanted to smack him in the nose. She moved to what she hoped was a bathroom when he spoke again.

"I don't think they want you to leave just yet. I'm pretty sure the police want to speak to you. I know my family wants to, as well. You saved our mother today."

He was probably related to the woman who'd tried to kill her. He didn't look like her, but she knew that it didn't matter. She didn't look a thing like her family either. She made her way to the door and was relieved it was indeed the bathroom.

She looked in the mirror and was surprised at the bruise around her neck. And even someone as novice as her about such things you could tell it was made with hands; fingerprints were evident even to her. Turning her head slightly, she could even make out the way her thumbs had dug into her windpipe. Turning her body around and opening the hospital gown, she looked at her back. There was a nice-sized bruise back there too, but not as bad. Joey had been able to deflect that one a little more.

Her arm had been wrapped up, and blood now seeped through the white gauze. There was some tape on her forehead and a little on her chin. She had no clue when she'd gotten those bumps, but figured it didn't matter. Joey didn't want to think about how much that was going to cost her, and she turned on the water. She was never going to get out of that stupid building.

She washed her face best she could and tried to figure out what had happened to her shirt and bra. There hadn't been a bag under the bed, and there was nothing in here either. She was going to end up stealing this thing to get home; she just knew it. Opening the door, she wasn't really surprised to see the man still there. But the police threw her a bit.

"Miss, we understand from your doctor that you can't speak much, but if you could tell us how you just happened to be in the building when it caught fire, we'll let you heal a little longer before we ask anything else."

She stared at the cop then at the man in the chair. He was looking at the cop too.

"You don't care that she has enough bruising around her neck to kill someone? You simply want to know how she was there to get them." It didn't sound to her like a question, which was good because handsome didn't give the cop time to answer. "Not to mention the fact that she did save two women from burning up in that same fire, and she did it at great risk to herself."

"Don't you think it's a bit convenient that she was there in the first place? I mean, maybe she was setting it up for some scam and didn't know that your mom was going to be in there. Or maybe she did." The cop looked over at her and smirked. "You could have been hoping for some reward money 'cause you saved her."

Joey took a step forward but was stopped when handsome stood up and shoved the guy against the wall. "Get out. Get out right now or, so help me, I'll call your captain right now and have him pick you up in a body bag."

She took a step back when the cop started toward her, and then another when the man raised his fist. Before she could wonder why he wanted to hit her, handsome intervened. Before she knew it, she was in the room alone. When the door opened again, handsome entered and was straightening his tie. Another man, equally as good-looking, was with him.

"You did not need to throw him down the hall. Mom is going to be pissed enough as it is." The second man looked at her and smiled. "Hello. My brother here tells me that you're leaving. I don't think you should either. You've been hurt, and you need care."

"No insurance," she said as she leaned against the bed. She was suddenly very exhausted and wanted nothing more than to crawl into bed and sleep. Both men shared a look and then walked toward her.

"We've got your bill, miss. You saved our mother, Annamarie, and it's the least we can do." Her rescuer picked her up and put her on the bed. She was settling down when man number two put the sheet over her. "Besides, Mom will be mad at us if we let you go before she has a chance to thank you yourself."

The door flew open, and a woman came in. She had a small bundle in her arms and nearly tossed it at the man who had come in with handsome. She was grabbing Joey into her arms before she could avoid her.

"She's all right. She said she was all right because of you." A little sob and another painful hug before she pulled away. "I don't know how to thank you."

"Letting her breathe would be a start, I bet."

The woman turned to handsome and glared at him.

"I'm just saying the girl probably hurts some, and you hugging her like you're doing could cause damage."

"Jesse Michael Hunter, you'll be nice to me, or I'll tell your mother about that girl from my house last week. You know the one."

Joey looked at the three of them. Hunter. All she could think about was that his name was Hunter. She must have made some sort of noise because they all turned to her, and she looked at the one she'd called Jesse.

"Jesse M. Hunter of Hunter Corporation?" He grinned and nodded. She closed her eyes and felt him come near her. "Stay away from me." Her throat felt on fire now, and she was dizzy. These people, at least the one who had thrown the cop out, were the reason she was homeless. Throwing off the covers again, she got out of the bed and went to the bathroom. She was going to be sick and didn't want them around when she was. She just got the door shut when her belly took its first lurch. She was on the floor seconds before she threw up the first time.

~~~

Jesse looked at his brother then at Kasey before he looked to where the girl had gone. He was going to ask what the hell happened when he heard her throwing up. The poor girl was going to hurt her throat more if she did that much more.

17

Royce asked him to step outside, and they left Kasey there in case the girl needed someone.

"What was that all about?"

Jesse didn't know and told him that.

"Well, do you have a name? Maybe a person to call if she has a family, husband?"

Jesse shook his head again. "I was going to ask her when robocop showed up and started to get nasty with her. Then you come in and now this. Do you think it's some sort of delayed reaction to the fire?"

Royce sighed and leaned against the wall. "I have no idea. She looked sort of sick when she found out your name. Do you think you did something to a friend of hers, and now she's pissed about it? Damn it, Jesse, how many times do I have to tell you to—"

Both men stood when the door opened. Jesse had been leaning against the nurses' station and Royce, the wall. The girl came out first, followed quickly by Kasey. And she didn't look all that happy either.

"I think you should come back in here. I know that the Hunter building will pay for your stay if that's what worries you." The girls fuck off made Jesse raise a brow, but Kasey wasn't finished. "It won't do you any good to get that cut infected. You should at least let someone give you a prescription or something for it."

Jesse moved after the girl and touched her shoulder to get her attention. He was flat on his back and staring at the ceiling before he could take a breath. Turning slightly, he watched as the girl moved down the hallway, her gown flapping in the wind. He looked up at Royce when he felt him standing over him. He wasn't thrilled to see him laughing.

"She may be hurting like hell, but she sure didn't have any problems throwing you to the floor." He leaned over laughing, and Jesse decided that he would gladly kill his older brother if it wasn't for the fact that he liked Kasey so much. "And damn it, for as long as I live, I'll never get the look on your face when you went over her like that from my mind."

Jesse didn't get up but lay there as everyone walked around him. He had to smile when he thought how he'd get back at his brother. He simply steepled his fingers over his chest and delivered his bomb. "You didn't help stop her, so you get to tell Mom that you let her get away." Just as he'd thought, Royce started to curse. "Yeah, you gonna kiss her with that mouth too?"

They were sitting in her room, waiting for their mom to wake when Daniel came in. He handed a file to Royce and kissed Kasey on her cheek. As soon as he sat down, Jesse started on him.

"I want you to look up all you can on someone. I don't have her name or anything, but I think she might have a grudge against me." Kasey laughed, and Royce handed him the folder. "She is a brunette with medium length to shortish hair, tall, and slightly underweight."

"Well, that should be a piece of cake," Daniel said sarcastically. "I can run a search on tall, skinny, dark-haired girls that you've pissed off."

"I didn't say I pissed her off, I said she might have a grudge against us, meaning the company, you moronic asshole." He flushed when he looked over at his sleeping mom. "And keep your voice down. You want to wake her up?"

They were all terrified of their mother. Not that she'd ever beaten them, though he was reasonably sure they each of them had deserved it a few times over in their lives. No, she frightened him because disappointing her was paramount to killing someone. And each of them hated to upset her in any way. She could make them feel ten again in a second.

He opened the file and looked at the aftermath of the fire. The building was gone, and even though they'd only thought about buying it, Jesse could still feel the waste of it. The fire trucks were still around when the photo he was holding had been taken, and when he started to flip it to the next one, he saw her. He stood up and handed it to Daniel.

"That's her. The girl that they're putting in the ambulance. Can you get that picture blown up?"

"Maybe. But I doubt it will be more than a blurry shot." He put the picture in his briefcase and leaned back in his chair. "Why do you want to know? Or is this some kind of matchup you're hoping to get?"

Royce started laughing, and Jesse knew he was going to tell how she'd gotten the better of him in the hall. He started to defend himself before that happened when their mother woke finally.

After reassuring them that she was fine, she asked about Sondra. "She needs to be found. I think she might have tried to hurt that girl who saved me. I couldn't believe it when she wouldn't help carry me out of the building."

"We don't know who the girl is. And I thought you told the police that she tried to help you out."

Royce looked at Curtis who'd had contact with the cops from the start.

"What did they say to you?"

"Not Sondra, the young girl. Have you talked to her yet?" No one made eye contact with her, and she grabbed him by the arm. "Jesse Michael, what did you do to her?"

"Me? I didn't do anything. She was already pi…mad when I got to her and trying to leave. The cop tried to insinuate that she'd set the fire for the reward. She left about half an hour ago." He realized what he'd told her seconds after he'd said it. He closed his eyes before opening them to look at her again. The look of anger surprised him, but the tight grip she had on his hand hurt.

"I told you to watch over her. Was that so hard for you to do?" She pinned Daniel with a look. "Did you find out about the building? Who owned it?"

"Yes, ma'am. It was bank owned and not insured. As far as I can tell, it was just an empty building without insurance. I did find a couple of things, something that didn't sink well, but I have my team looking into it."

"That girl saved me. She could have simply let me die when Sondra told her I was dead, but she didn't. She even went back in for the old fool when, by all accounts, the girl had already carried me to safety." She lay back on the bed. "Please find her for me. I need to thank her personally for helping me."

"I don't think she wants to be found," Kasey said quietly. "When she left, she was saying something about the fault of the Hunters, and that had she only stayed in her flophouse she'd not be in pain. I got the impression that she didn't like Jesse particularly."

He looked at his mom. He could see she hurt, but not at what she'd just heard. He, however, was mad enough for them both. "If you think I did anything to this girl, you're wrong. I don't have a single clue as to who she is. And as for finding her, I have a little bit to say to her as well."

Chapter 3

The cut on her arm was throbbing. She hadn't had a chance to look at it, but she was pretty sure that she'd pulled a few of the stitches out when she tossed Hunter to the floor. She grinned as she set another tray of dirty dishes through the washer. That had almost been worth it.

"Joe, there's some soup left if you want it. It's not a lot, but it will fill the void if you're hungry enough." She wasn't but nodded to Doyle O'Donnell, the owner, and cook. "And I put you a sandwich in the fridge for you to take home. Some jack wipe ordered it and didn't want it 'cause I put too much lettuce on it."

She knew that he was lying to her. If a customer had said that to him, Doyle would have popped him in the head with his baseball bat and told him to eat it anyway. He was that sort of guy. But he liked her, and he was the only person who knew she was homeless. He'd been having mistakes like this one more and more lately. She nodded, too emotional to say anything.

Letting the washer do its thing, she went to the table and sat down. As soon as her butt hit the chair, Doyle set a large bowl of chili in front of her and a sleeve of crackers. She normally didn't care for chili, but hunger wasn't picky. She started to eat and listen for the washer at the same time. When he slid a glass of milk in front of her with a terse, "drink it," she grinned and continued to eat.

"You're bleeding there." Doyle took her hand and turned over her arm to have a look. "You should get that checked out before your arm falls off. I don't have time for you to learn to wash the dishes one handed. You're slow enough as it is."

"It's fine." She took her arm back only to have him pull it back. "Don't, Doyle, it's fine."

She didn't watch as he cut away the gauze. Her stomach was already protesting over the pain. She thought if she looked, then all this good chili would come back up over both of them. She heard him hiss, but didn't ask. She knew it was bad.

"You're gonna have to go and get the stitches put back in, girl. You've opened all but a couple. Looks like you might have had as many as fifty here."

She glanced at the cut and jerked her head back. It was as bad as she thought. "I can't. I told you before that I can't afford a bill. Going back to get it fixed will only give them the opportunity to figure out I can't pay, and then I'll go to jail." She'd told him about the police and what they'd said about the fire. She hadn't told him about the Hunters. At least not this encounter with the Hunters. He did know about the apartment building.

He got up and came back with a first aid kit. "You'd think somebody'd be a little happy that no one died in that fire rather than complain that you didn't hang around to file no report for them."

She only nodded. She couldn't speak, not while he was

24

probing at her arm like he was. Sweat poured off her face, and she knew that any second she was going to faint from it. Leaning her head on the table, she tried taking deep breaths, but all it did was make the scent of blood fill her mouth. Jumping up and holding her hand over her mouth, she ran to the bathroom.

She could hear Doyle cussing on the other side of the door. It might have made her laugh any other time, but she was seriously trying to hold onto herself. When she was emptied of her dinner, she sat on the cold floor and thought about her life.

Her parents were both dead. She'd not been overly close to them anyway, but she missed them at times. They had both died in a plane crash when she'd been about fifteen. So she'd lived with her grandmother, her dad's mom, until she turned eighteen. It had only been three years but had seemed thirty. The day she'd turned old enough to be on her own, she left and hadn't been back since.

She'd wanted to go to college and had for a few years, but money was tight, and she couldn't always afford the books required. After getting most of a forestry degree, she'd had to drop out. Then when she'd landed a job working in a nursery, she thought she was going to be able to get her degree. But Mother Nature decided to deal her a different set of cards.

A freak storm, they'd called it. Hail the size of baseballs had broken nearly every pane of glass in the old greenhouse. And if that wasn't enough, every one of the newly planted flowers and vegetables that she'd moved to the sales floor the night before had lain broken and dying when the storm passed. The Hamiltons, owners of the nursery, had been devastated. And the insurance company waited just long enough to pay them off that the business had been ruined and any chances of a career she might have had. They retired to Florida, where they could finish out their years living off their kids. After giving her five hundred dollars bonus, they left the day after the check cleared.

After that, each time she started to get a little ahead, something would happen. The apartment she lived in, the refrigerator had broken down. The landlord said it wasn't his, so he wasn't going to replace it. The stove stopped working; again, she had to pay for the repairs. Mrs. Rivers didn't have the full amount for her rent two months in a row because her worthless son had taken her retirement checks. The list was endless, and here she sat on a semi-clean floor feeling sorry for herself. She flushed the toilet and got up.

Dizziness swamped her, but she simply held on until it passed. She couldn't afford to go to the hospital any more than she could afford to lose her job. Washing her mouth out and covering her arm as best she could with paper towels, she went back to the kitchen. There was a mug sitting in place of the soup, and she could see that along with the first aid kit was a large, white towel and some bottles of meds. She moved toward the dishwasher when Doyle caught her.

"Sit," he commanded. "If you won't go to the hospital, then I bring it to you. Missy is coming over. She works at the clinic. She said she'd stitch you up tonight, but tomorrow you come see her." Joey opened her mouth to protest, and he glared at her. She shut up with a snap of her teeth. "Good girl. Now sit and drink that broth. It's beef. You need the vitamins."

She didn't have the heart to tell him she didn't think it would stay down either but sipped at it until the nurse showed up. She taped the wound closed, telling her that she needed to clean it first before she'd stitch it and complained to Doyle the whole time about his dirty table. When he walked away grumbling about women and their need to have everything spotless, she winked at Joey. At least she thought she winked. The pills she'd given her were making her feel decidedly slappy...happy.

"He's such a big baby. Nearly cried when he called me to tell me you're hurt. He has a tender heart for those he considers friends."

Joey nodded but didn't say anything. She was suddenly fascinated with watching the little strips of tape being put on her arm.

An hour later, she was lying on the floor of the bar she worked at. Doyle had wanted to take her home, but she didn't know how to tell him she couldn't find her buttonholes much less her flop, so he'd given her the blanket he'd had in his car and told her to sleep it off. She thought maybe she was asleep before he turned off the lights.

~~~

Jesse was in his office when Curtis walked in. He'd spent most of last night on a security issue in the building and had finally had to call Kasey in to help. She was his assistant, but in reality, she knew the building better than he did.

"Mom comes home tomorrow morning. Her lungs are clear, and her ribs are healing nicely." Curtis sat in his chair and propped his feet on his desk as he continued. "I've had someone looking for anyone to fit the description of the girl. I thought maybe she might live close to the fire. Turns out I was right."

Jesse wanted to ask about what he'd found out but also

knew from years of being his brother that if he asked, he'd get nothing. So he continued to write his report on the missing lunches that Kasey had helped him with.

"She went to the clinic this morning. They're putting in the stitches again, as we speak." Jesse looked up at his brother. "I thought you'd like to go with me to see her."

Jesse leaned back in his chair, knowing there was a catch. "And you came to me because…"

Grinning, he dropped his feet to the floor and stood. "I thought maybe if I took you, then you'd piss her off again, and I'd get to see her throw your ass to the floor. Think you can arrange it for me?"

With a very heartfelt, "fuck off," Jesse grabbed his coat. He was standing at the elevator, waiting on it to open when Curtis came up beside him and handed him a file. There wasn't a name, but he opened it anyway. A bloodied arm was the first thing he saw.

"Christ, Curtis, a little warning next time." He stepped into the opening as he thumbed through the other pictures. "Is this her arm or are you perverted about open wounds?"

"Hers. She thinks these were taken for a school assignment. The nurse working at the clinic took them and sent them to me ten minutes ago. She said the girl was in a great deal of pain but refused any drugs."

The cut was long and nasty-looking. There were some strips of tape being removed like someone had tried to close it that way. The ten or so pictures showed the wound in various stages of the tape being removed, then the stitches being put in. The last picture showed the open gash in her arm and a profile of the girl.

"Did she give a name?"

Curtis shook his head.

"Then how are they treating her without some sort of background information."

He knew as soon as he asked. It was a clinic, not a hospital. And the one where they were headed was known for treating druggies and other issues that weren't high on the list of getting valid information.

"The student nurse said she thought maybe the girl was a friend of the woman who runs the clinic. She said she thought maybe she'd been the one who'd put it back together. The girl, the one from the fire, asked about having her leg looked at too. Something about a burn. Did you know she'd been burned at the fire?"

He hadn't, but it wouldn't have surprised him to know that she had been burned. The fire was massive, and firefighters were still at the scene, putting out smaller explosions that still went off. The building had been storing chemicals that hadn't been removed when the owners had moved out.

They drove over instead of using the limo. This place wasn't in the best of neighborhoods, and the limo would draw unwanted attention. They pulled in the lot twenty minutes after Curtis had come into his office.

The building had seen better days. The paint was peeling off in, not strips, but in hunks. Jesse thought if the building was still standing this time next year, he'd be surprised. But when they entered, he was taken aback. The place was immaculate.

Plants lined the wall behind the counter, and the walls were a bright white. He glanced at the magazines on the little table they passed, and he could see that they were current, unlike the ones in his own doctor's office. The girl behind the counter must have been the one that Curtis had been speaking to as she nodded them through with a low "four" as they passed.

With a short, hard knock, Curtis entered the little room first. Jesse could see someone lying on a bed with her back to him and another woman, this one dressed all in white, saying something to her.

"I know you can't really hear me, love, but I want you to take a deep breath, honey, and I'll get this cleaned for you. Why those idiots left this unattended is beyond me." Without taking her eyes from her patient, she barked at who she thought had entered the room. "Bring me some more four-by-fours, darling. This is much worse than I thought."

When the nurse or doctor moved, Jesse could see it was indeed bad. She turned to them then and stared. Before she could speak, the door behind them opened.

"She's been out for over an hour, but I still like to think they can hear me. I want you to call an ambulance and have them come and get her." Jesse turned to see who was there and saw that the girl from the desk was there. "And if you had anything to do with these two in here, you're fired."

Curtis spoke first. "Don't fire her. It's my fault. This girl is important to my family as she saved my mom the day before yesterday. We've been looking for her to see if she's alright."

"Well, as you can see, she's not. I don't know what kind of dumb ass it was that treated her, but he should be barred from treating animals much less humans."

"What did you give her? I thought...what did you give her to knock her out?" Jesse flushed when the doctor looked at him. "She left the hospital before treatment could be finished. But I agree, someone should have seen this."

30

The burn on the back of her leg was horrific. It was at least eight inches long and nearly half as wide. The blister had burst at some point, and it now seeped with puss. He could also see that there were bits of something in the wound, and he didn't want to think what it was. The doctor explained before his imagination got the better of him.

"She's been wearing her jeans over it without protection. It's gotten infected, and she needs to get some antibiotics in her. I don't know how much longer she would have gone if I hadn't seen her last night and insisted she come here to have me stitch up her arm. Poor thing was working through her shift when my friend called me after she'd thrown up her dinner and started bleeding."

Jesse nodded. He didn't ask what was on the tip of his tongue. The woman was helping them. He didn't want to piss her off, asking why she didn't have an ambulance called last night. He could hear the sirens even as he looked at his watch. Curtis stepped out as he moved toward the head of the girl.

She was covered in sweat, and he looked up at the doctor to ask. Again, she answered before he spoke. "She passed out from the pain, I would imagine. She was in a great deal of it last night, and I would guess it didn't get any better her walking here from the bar."

"What bar?" He wasn't sure why he cared but would file away the information in the event that she left again without him getting her name.

"Doyle's on tenth. She does dishes a few nights a week he told me and when she can, works the bar for him. Doyle said she's had a bit of bad luck lately, and he likes the girl."

Jesse nodded. "You know where she lives?" She shook her head. He didn't think she would. "How about her name?"

He looked up when she cleared her throat.

"You know who tried to strangle her?"

He nodded.

"Anyone I can help along to an early grave?"

"I'm working on that myself." He looked at the girl and brushed her damp hair from her cheek. "My mother has friends in high places and is working on a campaign to get that to work as we speak."

"I love your mom then. All I know about her name is she goes by 'Joey.' Doyle thinks her last name might be Foster, but he's not sure. I think he's lying about that. She hasn't been all that forthcoming, so he said. I think he's trying to protect her."

It was more than he'd had. Further conversation was stopped when two medics arrived. He realized when one of them called her Missy that he'd not asked her name. Jesse made a mental note to make a sizeable donation to this clinic to help keep her working here. Her licenses were hanging on the wall next to the door, and he noticed that she'd graduated from Harvard. And that her last name was Cummings.

Jesse shook Missy's hand as Joey was being loaded. She'd made it so he could ride along with her. Curtis was following in the car. Jesse had no idea what he was going to say to Joey if she woke and started asking questions, but he was more concerned by the way the medics had worked on her. Her temp had spiked, they said, and they worked very hard to get it to go down.

Chapter 4

Annamarie watched the girl sleep. She'd gotten out of surgery more than three hours ago, and the surgeon had said he wasn't worried when she didn't wake when he'd projected.

"She's been fighting off the infection for several days. If she wakes before morning at this point, I'll be surprised. The girl is strong, I'll give her that." He'd ordered her pain medications to be given every four hours to keep her still and told Annamarie that she could stay with the girl until she was tossed out.

She snorted. As much money as the Hunters donated to this hospital yearly, they should name the sucker after her. She closed her eyes and thought about the girl, woman really that lay so still on the bed.

Her name was Josephine Delilah Foster, twenty-six, and the only child of Mary and Donald Foster. It was probably just as well she'd been their only child. By all accounts, they hadn't cared much for the one they had. She'd been living with a grandmother who seemed more inclined to get loaded up on Friday night and stay that way until Friday morning of the next week. She's gone through what little money the younger couple had left their daughter in less than a year. And had

33

treated Josephine like a live-in maid more than a grandchild. When she'd turned eighteen, less than four years later, the young Joey had moved around a great deal. It wasn't until she'd moved into the Buster Apartments that she'd begun to make some headway into getting herself some sort of life. Annamarie turned when the door opened behind her.

"What have you found out?" She whispered the question to her son. "I know we own the building she lived in, but I'm thinking there might be more to the story than we'd been told."

Daniel shifted in his chair, uncomfortable. She was sure that whatever he had to tell her wasn't going to be good.

"We bought the building about two years ago. We'd been trying to work with the previous owner, but he was being evasive. He told us, according to the report that Royce filed with the building, that the people wouldn't cooperate. Then when we still had tenants after the required ninety days, we gave them another four extensions. He was handling the evictions for us."

Annamarie looked back at the girl on the bed when she stirred. "You think he let them know what was going on?"

"No. I looked in the file and found a few letters. Some of them were from someone on the tenants' group, and a few of them were from her." He nodded to the girl and handed her some letters. "She claimed that they hadn't been given enough time. That there were people in the building that were going to have to move to nursing homes. Conway, the owner, said she was a pain in the ass, and he backed his story up about her being nuts with a few letters from her neighbors. We just simply let him handle it as this was about the time we were going to court over that thing with Kasey."

34

Annamarie nodded. Yes, they'd been all pretty devastated over the things that had come about when Kasey had worked for them. And now they were about to have another go with the press.

She opened the letters and only glanced at them. Her head still hurt from the blow she'd taken when she'd been knocked off her feet at the fire. She gave them back to Curtis. She just wanted to crawl into her bed and rest. She opened her eyes and looked at her son. "Jesse. Do you know what the relationship between him and this girl is about? I heard they had words in the hospital before she left the first time." She'd laughed at the story that Kasey had told her about the woman and her son. "Do you think he likes her?" Curtis didn't answer, so she asked again.

"Are you playing matchmaker, Mom? If so, I don't want any part of it. She's just a good kid that's been dealt some pretty nasty crap. Thank her for saving your life and leave her alone."

Annamarie didn't say anything right away, too mad at Curtis for thinking her so devious. It didn't really matter that he was partly right; she just didn't like him knowing it. "The girl deserves a break. And, if at all possible, I'd like for him to keep away from her. She doesn't need him breaking her heart because he wants to screw her." She was happy to see that she shocked him and turned her head away from him before he could see her smile. "You make sure that he is aware that she is off limits to him, or he will answer to me."

A few minutes later, a nurse came in to tell Curtis that he had a phone call. His cell had been turned off, and the caller needed to speak to him. Curtis left her alone once again. A few minutes later, Joey rolled to her back and spoke.

35

"I don't know who you are, but you'd better have a damned good reason for bringing me back to the hospital that I can't afford." She groaned when she moved again. "And my flipping throat still hurts." With that, she burst into tears. Annamarie got up and went to her, asking her to please cover her eyes so that she could turn on the light. With the light on, Annamarie fussed with the bedside table while Joey got control again. After a few minutes, the girl thanked her.

"I need you to see if they can get me a set of the A.M.A. papers. I think they have them on file at the nurses' station. I'm sure if you tell them I don't have any insurance, they'll get them right away."

"You can't leave against medical advice for lack of insurance. Well, I suppose you could, but that doesn't matter." Annamarie smiled at her.

"I'm sure it might not matter to you, but this place frowns upon you not being able to pay your bill. And I can't." She stared at her for several seconds before she spoke again. "You're the lady from the building. Hunter. You're Mrs. Hunter."

Had Annamarie not been looking at her, she would have missed the change. Her entire face seemed to tense up, and she could feel the hostility boiling off her. She stiffened and pulled herself to the other side of the bed.

"I need for you to go away now. I'm glad you're okay, but I don't want to have anything to do with you people."

Curtis walked in just then and started to say something to Joey that Annamarie thought might not be very nice.

"You have every right to be mad at the Hunters for what we've apparently done to you. If I were in your shoes, I'd be pissy about it too. That's why I want to make this up to you

36

any way I can."

"You can make it up to me by getting your rich ass out of my room. I don't need, nor do I want, your charity." Joey pulled on the call cord so hard she yanked it from the wall.

When Curtis started to help her, Annamarie stopped him with a look. "Curtis, please go and get your brother. I think Jesse has something to say to her, as well. And bring Kasey. She should have what I asked to get for me."

Joey didn't move until the nurse came in. She simply handed her the broken cord, told her how sorry she was, and asked if she could please have a copy of the A.M.A. paperwork.

The nurse looked at Annamarie, and she nodded. She could have them, but she wasn't leaving. Not like this anyway. She sat in the chair again and waited for the cavalry. Curtis returned first, then Kasey and Jesse. He didn't even speak to her but went straight to the girl.

"You look better. How are you feeling?" Joey answered by growling at him, and it was everything she could do not to laugh at her son. "I guess your throat still hurts. The doc said it might be a few more days before it felt better."

When the nurse came in and handed her the papers, Jesse snatched them right up. He was walking away from the bed as he read them. Annamarie watched as Kasey brought Joey the bag.

"I got you some clothes. It took us a while to figure out where you lived. It was very cozy, by the way. Much better than my first apartment. Anyway, most of your things were gone. I figured someone noticed you weren't around, so they took what was there. Your bed and things had been ransacked, and we think some transient might have found it before we did."

"I'm a transient, in case you hadn't noticed. And I don't want your clothes. I have…I have things I can get my hands on if I need them." Everyone in the room could see the hurt on her face when she'd found out about her things. "And will you please give me back those forms?"

"I don't think so," Jesse said as he sat on the couch. "These say you're leaving against medical advice. The only way you're getting out of that bed is if I carry you somewhere or you're released by a certified doctor."

Curtis cleared his throat and asked to speak to Jesse in the hall. This is where either the fireworks began, or Jesse walked away. Either way, she was prepared. Annamarie was slightly disappointed when Curtis came back in alone but brightened when Jesse came in a few minutes later. He seemed tense, and she was nearly giddy with happiness. This could be a turning point in both his and Joey's lives.

"I am trying to be very nice. Extremely nice, as a matter of fact, but I have had enough." Joey took a deep breath and continued. "I want you people to get the fuck out of here and give me back my paperwork."

No one moved. Joey picked up the pillow, and before she could throw it if that had been her intention, Jesse took it from her. Annamarie was nervous then. She nearly told her son she was sorry before he spoke.

"I would like a word with Miss Foster. If you all wouldn't mind waiting outside, I'll be quick. What I have to say to her won't take but a couple of minutes." She started to protest, but he simply guided her to the door. "I won't be a minute, I promise."

She was out in the hall a few scant seconds later. She

looked over at Curtis, and he sat beside her on the bench that was just outside of Joey's room. She asked him what had happened between him and his brother.

"He said he will pursue who he wants when he wants, and I was to keep my...nose out of it." Curtis grinned. "He had a different viewpoint when I told him you had said so. But I think you're wrong about this."

She looked at him, waiting for him to continue. When he didn't, she asked, "Wrong about what? You want him to hurt her? I don't. She saved my life and probably Sondra's, even though I think the woman tried to kill the poor child. What would you have me say?"

He never answered because Jesse came out of the room just then. Well, she supposed stormed would have been a better description. He didn't even speak but stomped past them. He dropped some wadded up papers into the trashcan at the desk as he swept by it. Both her and Curtis stood and went to Joey's room. Annamarie was afraid she'd gone too far this time.

~~~

Joey watched the door open slowly. She knew that it wouldn't have been Mr. Hunter again. She was pretty sure he'd said all he had to say. She took several deep breaths to try to control herself, especially in light of who walked in. Mrs. Hunter and another Mr. Hunter. She should have figured there'd be a round two.

"Are you all right, dear?"

Joey nodded, afraid to speak.

"Did he hurt you? I can make him come back and—"

"I'm fine. Peachy." She didn't want him back. This time, he might hit her. She'd never seen a man so pissed before.

"I'd like to be alone if you don't mind. I'm sort of tired." She waited for her to tell her that she was staying. Curtis, this Mr. Hunter, simply nodded and picked up his coat that had been across the chair. He cleared his throat before he said anything. She didn't know why, but she thought he was trying to think of how to tell her something.

"Are you really all right, Miss Foster?"

She nodded, then turned away. The tears were burning.

"Good then. The desk has my phone number if you need anything. My wife and I will get you whatever you need."

She nodded again. When the door closed, she turned and saw that Mrs. Hunter hadn't left with her son. She didn't sit but held her coat. Joey hoped that she'd simply go too.

"Are you going to leave as soon as I walk out the door?"

She shook her head, then answered. "No, ma'am. I'm here until...until I'm released officially." She didn't add that she either stayed or would have to pay the bill in full and then face the wrath of Mr. Jesse M. Hunter.

Mrs. Hunter nodded. She turned away then back to face her. "What did Jesse say to you? Did he threaten you? I won't have him bully you, Joey. I will speak to him."

"I'm very tired, Mrs. Hunter. And your son didn't...he didn't bully me. I swear to you." Joey rolled to her side and closed her eyes. "Goodbye, Mrs. Hunter."

The door closed with a soft click. Joey didn't move for long moments, afraid that she had fooled her again. Joey reached up and turned off the light, then lay there in the darkness and wondered how she'd ever thought that doing the right thing could fuck up your life so badly.

Chapter 5

Curtis watched his brother pace. It had been nearly twenty-four hours since Josephine Foster had been admitted to the hospital the second time, and he was pretty sure Jesse was going to explode soon. He'd done everything but pull out a gun and start shooting things in his office.

"When do we get the results from the fire? I would have thought with your pull, you'd have had them by now." Curtis handed him the file again. "What took you so long to mention this?"

He plopped down in the chair across from Curtis' desk and didn't open the file. Again. He decided that he was going to give him five more minutes of this mood, then he was either going to leave him in his office or beat the shit out of him. The latter was sounding better and better.

"Have you spoken to her?"

The question startled Curtis, and it took him a few seconds to gear away from the bloody mess he was going to make of Jesse's face. "Who? Joey?"

Jesse nodded.

"No. She knows how to reach me if she needs anything."

Curtis didn't mention that other than a daily report from

41

the nurse he had hired for the girl, she'd not spoken to a soul. At least during the day. A friend of hers, the bartender Doyle, came by when Curtis assumed the bar closed and left around six in the morning. He was also bringing her food.

"She's supposed to be released in a few days, I guess. The doctor said that night that she'd be there for a week or so. He wanted to make sure her cuts healed, and the infection was gone."

Curtis only nodded. Actually, she was getting out in the morning, a full four days early. But if Jesse didn't ask, Curtis didn't see any reason to tell him. Kylie thought he was being mean, but did like the idea of Jesse not having control over something.

Curtis sat up and handed his brother another file. "Sondra Jennings hasn't been heard from at either her apartment nor her work. I'm pretty sure she realizes by now that Mom or the police are looking for her. Frankly, I hope she stays hidden. The insurance company is also looking for her. The company she works for is as well."

He opened the file and stared at it. Curtis was hoping his brother would take some interest in something other than the girl. He didn't know what Jesse had said to her, but he was pretty sure whatever it had been was eating at him.

"It says here that there was an insurance policy taken out on the building. Is that normal for them?" Curtis nodded, waiting for him to get to the good part. "Miss Jennings is the benefactor?"

"Now that's *not* normal. They have it insured in the event that someone gets hurt during a showing. Something like we do when we purchase a building. But in this case, not only did the agency take out one, but so did Jennings. Hers took effect the week before the agencies did." Curtis pulled out a few sheets of paper he'd not added to the file yet. "According to the records, her brother-in-law owned that building before the bank took it. There are several more he'd had to file over. It looks to me like she was trying to help him recoup his losses."

Jesse opened the file over his desk now and was reading it. Curtis knew his security instincts would kick in, and he watched him get absorbed in the project.

"It says here that Jennings and Sons owned nine of the nineteen buildings in the area. You think the police are looking into those as well?" Jesse looked up when Curtis' phone rang. He glanced at the caller ID and almost let it go to voice mail. Damn, but the girl had timing.

"Hello, Curtis Hunter here." The pause at the other end didn't bother him. He knew she'd not hung up. There were the distinct sounds of a hospital going on in the background.

"I'm getting released now. The doctor has said it was alright. I need a fax number to send the paperwork to, or I can't leave. Your brother made that perfectly clear." Curtis glanced at his brother and wondered again what he'd said to Joey.

"I can give you one. Do you have a pen?" When she said she did, he told her the number to the one in his office. "When are you sending it?"

"He said he'd send it over now. I won't leave until I hear back from somebody on your end." He waited, knowing she had more to say. "He will find out, won't he? You'll let him know you got it, so I'm clear?"

Anger and something more was in her voice. Something he couldn't tell over the phone, but it sounded like she was hurt. And her not telling Jesse herself was telling as well.

"Yes. I'll make sure he knows. Do you have an address yet?" Jesse stood up and leaned into the phone to listen. Curtis didn't even try to stop him.

"That wasn't part of the orders. I'll expect to hear from you when you get it. Goodbye." She hung up as Jesse jerked the phone from him.

"That was her, Miss Foster."

Curtis nodded.

"You told me that you'd not heard from her."

"I hadn't. That's the first time since... What did you say to her? That night in the hospital room? What did you say to her that made her think that you'd threatened her in some way to have to stay until she was officially released?"

Jesse flushed and returned to his seat. "Nothing. I didn't actually threaten her. Not really. I simply told her that she'd either stay until she was released or she'd pay the entire hospital bill. Including Mom's bill."

Curtis took two deep breaths before he thought he could speak without killing Jesse. "You threatened her. No matter how you try to butter it up so it looks good, you threatened that poor girl. No wonder she won't have anything to do with..." Curtis stood up and grabbed his coat.

"Where do you think you're going? If you think I'm going to allow you to go to the hospital and see that—"

He'd hit his brother before. When they'd been kids, once or twice maybe, and when they'd been in their late teens, but never as an adult. And he wasn't sure what had driven him to hit him now. But he did. His fist was connecting with Jesse's face before he could blink. And when he tumbled over the chair behind him, Curtis was right there standing over him, daring him to get up.

"You. Do. *Not*. Allow. Me. To. Go. Anywhere. Do I make myself perfectly clear? And if this is the way you spoke to Joey, it's small wonder she is acting like we're the enemy." Curtis stretched his neck before continuing. "You fucking asshole, if you come near that girl, I will castrate you myself."

When Curtis turned to leave, his secretary, as well as his mother and brother, were standing there. He glanced back at his brother, who still lay on the floor, and continued to the door. When Royce opened his mouth, Curtis told him to ask the prick. He didn't even say he was sorry to his mom as he walked to the elevator.

~~~

Joey looked at the television again. The little clock in the corner kept moving. It was not forty minutes since she'd been told the fax had gone through, and nothing. She was going to call the office again but didn't want to unless she absolutely had to. She didn't know why, but she thought that Curtis had been trying to hide the fact that she was on the phone from someone and she just knew it was going to be Jesse.

She looked over at her friend and boss, Doyle. He was reading, and she smiled at the cover. *Moby Dick*. He might look uneducated, but under those tattoos and bald head lay the heart of a philosopher.

He looked up at her and winked. "That Melville sure knew how to tell a story." He stretched out his huge frame. "I'm not in any hurry, girly. I got the bar covered if I'm not back, and besides, it's Tuesday night. No football on. Now, if this was Monday? Hell, girly, you'd be getting yourself home by bus."

She was still laughing when the door opened. Finally, she thought and smiled. But when she saw who was there, she

45

felt it slide from her face. She just knew the Hunters were here to take another pound of her flesh.

"That's very telling." Curtis came into the room with a beautiful woman right behind him. She was hugely pregnant. "This is my wife, Kylie. And before you ask, no, she's not in labor."

"I wasn't. Why are you here? I kept my end of the bargain. You can't renege now." She flushed when she realized how rude she was being. "I'm sorry. I just want out of this."

"You're free to go. I have some things I'd like to ask you if you don't mind." She watched him open a briefcase that he'd set on the bedside table. "Just some questions about what happened."

"What's this going to cost me?" She looked over at Doyle when he growled at her to behave. Again, she flushed.

"Nothing but a little bit of your time." He was helping his wife sit as he answered. She watched how tender he was being with her and how he looked at her with such emotion. He caught her looking at them, and he winked.

What was wrong with everyone today, she wondered? In less than ten minutes, she'd been winked at twice. She had gone her entire life without a single one. And now, a married man and…well, and Doyle.

She had to get away from them. She'd spent the last year all alone with only Doyle as her friend, and now there were all sorts of people wanting to be chummy to her. Getting up, she limped her way to the bathroom with a hasty "be back" said over her shoulder.

She wiped at the tears. Joey didn't know what the hell was wrong with her, but every time she thought she had a handle, she'd break down again. It was that man, that bastard that had done this. He'd hurt her, humiliated her too. He'd treated her as though she was nothing, less than nothing.

Joey could hear the voices on the other side of the door, but couldn't make out the words. She knew that Doyle thought she was going to stay with him and his mom, but she had no intention of doing that. Joey knew Mrs. O'Donnell disliked her and wasn't going to have the woman treating Doyle badly because she was there.

She knew that the woman was very ill and that Doyle was caring for her, but man, the woman was caustic. Giggling a little, Joey realized she was too and wondered briefly if that was why they didn't care for each other. She wiped again at her face and opened the door.

"Fuck," she said before she could stop it. And when the pregnant Mrs. Hunter laughed, all hopes of thinking they might not have heard flew out the window. She walked to her bed and began putting her things in the bag that the hospital had given her.

"I would like to speak to you if you don't mind."

She glanced at Jesse and didn't answer.

"Please, Miss Foster. I would like to tell you how sorry —"

"Sorry doesn't cut it, you fucking jackass. You treated me like scum. Worse than scum, you treated me like I was beneath you. I probably am, but there was no reason for you to point it out to me." She stuffed the shirt she'd come in into the bag. "Telling me that I couldn't leave here because you were the high and mighty Jesse M. Hunter, like I didn't fucking know that."

"I did not act high and might —"

"I'm speaking here. You had your chance, and now it's my turn. Where was I? Oh, yeah. The high and mighty Jesse

M. Hunter said I was to stay put like I was a dog, and he was making me obey." She turned to him and poked him in the chest with her finger. "I'm not a dog. I'm not a doormat either. For that matter, I'm pretty fucking amazing if you want to know."

"I'm beginning to see that."

She didn't know why his smile pissed her off more, but it did. She was on a roll now and wasn't letting him off the hook just yet. "You acted like I'd hurt your mom and said I was to be nice to her, respect her, or I'd pay. Respect is earned, you moron, or haven't you ever heard that? And be nice? Who the fuck do you think went in that burning building after her? Me. I did that. If that wasn't being nice to her, then I don't know what the hell you want." She'd backed him against the wall, and when he'd flipped her around so that she was now backed up and he in front of her, she saw that the room was empty. She closed her mouth with a snap. She was so dead.

"May I speak now?"

She nodded, afraid to say anything more.

"Thank you. You were right. I was an asshole. And a moron, and everything else you called me. Including a prick."

"I didn't call you a prick." She didn't think she had, not to his face anyway. "I said you were the other things, but not that."

"I am, though, aren't I?"

She didn't answer, thinking there was a catch somewhere. She pushed at his chest. She thought he was simply too close for comfort. He, however, didn't move. "You're going to have to back up." He spread his hands wide against the wall on either side of her waist. She swallowed hard and tried again. "I can't breathe when you're this close to me. Please back up."

Instead of moving away, he seemed to move closer. Her heart felt like it was pounding, and she was sure he could hear it. She tried again to push at him and, when she put her hands over his chest, he covered her hands with one of his.

"I'd like to show you how sorry I am." His voice had taken on a different timbre, low, soft, and a little sexy. "Will you let me show you, Josephine?"

"It's Joey, and you'll have to back up if you want to show me anything. Right now, you couldn't get a piece of paper between us." She barely recognized her own voice as it sounded a lot like his. "Please?"

"Gladly." His mouth swept over hers softly. His touch was so brief and soft that if she couldn't still feel his breath on her lips, she'd swear it never happened. The second time he did it, he nibbled on her lower lip, worried it a bit before he pulled back. She heard a small whimper and thought it was her, but wasn't sure.

"Mr. Hunter, you need to back up. I don't think this is a good idea." This time when she touched his chest, she didn't push at him. In fact, she seemed to have no control over her fingers wrapping into his jacket. "You have to…you need to…"

"I agree. It's time to finish…or start." His mouth took hers. And when he wrapped his fingers in her hair and tilted her head, she felt his tongue enter her mouth and devastate her, taste her, and, Christ, it felt like he claimed her.

Chapter 6

The kiss wasn't enough. He'd had no idea a woman could taste so delicious and sexy at the same time. Moving himself more flush with her body, he groaned when she rocked her hips into his. Jesse cupped her ass and brought her against his cock.

He'd only meant to kiss her, a simple brush of his mouth over hers. He'd been an ass, the jackass that she'd called him, and he wanted to tell her that he wasn't. But her mouth looked so lush and inviting that he'd not been able to stop himself from having a taste. But a taste wasn't enough.

Jesse wanted to tell her he was sorry, that he'd been more worried about her than he'd been about any living thing in his life. He wanted to help her, hold her, and mostly he wanted to bury himself deep inside of her. Shifting again, he palmed her breast and felt her heart pounding. He captured her moan and her soft sigh.

He lifted his head when he felt something. His belly lurched, then his breath. He tried to let go of her, but his fingers suddenly wouldn't cooperate. Even when she whimpered, he simply held on. Taking a step back, then another, he knew she'd kneed him; his balls and cock knew it too.

Even as he dropped to the floor, his body curled around itself. His hand instinctively cupped his now softening erection, trying to protect what she'd already injured. He looked up at her as pain exploded over him, from the top of each hair follicle to the tips of his toes.

"Why?" he whispered through the pain. She didn't move and he couldn't. They stared at each other for several seconds before he realized she was crying. Jesse wanted to comfort her, but he couldn't move. She stepped over him at last, and, grabbing up the bag, she left the room.

It was probably only a few seconds before the door opened again. He prayed that she was coming back to finish him off. But he knew that he couldn't be that lucky. He knew that when he heard his brothers laughing, he'd never live this down even if he lived to be a hundred.

"She sent us in here because she said you fell. I'm thinking she just wanted to give us something to laugh about after she kicked your balls up around your ears." Royce laughed harder as he knelt down to peer into his face. "Did she hurt you anywhere else? Should we check to see if she stabbed you while you were...down?"

In that moment, Jesse decided that he could easily kill his older brother. Jesse decided the next time his brother needed something from him, even if it was a dollar to buy a paper, he was going to make him pay. In his pain-laced mind that had made sense, but when he'd said as much to Royce, it sounded as stupid as his brother apparently thought it was.

As he lay there while the pain receded, he heard his mom come in. He didn't even bother trying to explain. To everyone else, including her, it was obvious what had happened. But unlike what he was sure they were thinking, he'd not forced

see Josephine, then I will. *If* we decide to have seven kids out of wedlock, then we will. But you, my dear lady, will stay out of it. Do you know why?"

"Because you think you're an adult. And you think you know better. Well, I've decided that I'll tell you what they find out and maybe keep you informed, but if you hurt her or she hurts you…then I'm going to tell you I told you so until I'm pushing up daisies."

He kissed her cheek. "Agreed. Now, I think I'll go and buy some protection and see if she and I can have wild sex." He was still grinning at her expression as he left the hospital. He felt really good about what had just happened. He'd had the last word. Now he needed to figure out who Daniel had been watching over Josephine and figure out where she was.

~~~

Joey watched the man walking behind her in the shop windows as she passed them. She was sure he was following her, but for the life of her, couldn't figure out why. She thought about stopping and confronting him, but his size scared her a little. Next time she went out job hunting, she was taking something to protect herself with.

That's when she remembered the perfume in her bag. She hated the smell and had decided to dispose of it as soon as she could. But it had kept finding its way to the bottom of her bag, and every time she touched it reaching for something else, she'd remember that she had to drop it off in a trash can. Now she reached in the seemingly bottomless pit she called a purse and couldn't find it.

Ah ha, she thought when she wrapped her fingers around it and was happy to notice that the cap had come off. Pressing the little tab, she smelled the noxious odor coming from her left hand and figured she had the thing pointed away from her hand. Good, when she had to deploy it, she wouldn't end up with a face full of the crap.

Stopping in a window to look at the mannequins there, she pretended to shop. Though why anyone would want to wear the thing was beyond her. Glancing at the price tag, she nearly laughed out loud. Seriously? Did people actually pay three thousand dollars for a stupid dress that looked like it was made out of plastic? And those shoes? Really? The heels alone would cause painful feet, and then there was the —

The man moved within ten feet, and she decided to pretend she was going inside. Going to the deep doorway, she hid just around the corner and waited. It didn't take long for the big man to come near her, and she sprayed him as soon as he reached for the handle of the shop.

"Mother fucking son of a bitch, that fucking hurts." He started to rub at the liquid on his face and danced around too. "What the fuck, Miss Foster? Did you have to try and blind me?"

She held up the bottle again and advanced toward him. "How did you know my name? And why are you following me?"

He stopped so suddenly that she was afraid he was faking it to get to her. She looked around, just realizing that he could have a partner. He held up his hands and backed up.

"My name is Jared Stone. The man with me, the coward who is still on the other side of the street," he yelled. "That's my brother-in-law Alex. Alexander James, and we're not here to hurt you."

"Then you're a pervert? You like scaring helpless women on the street?" She waved the bottle at Alex as he came toward her and nearly tossed it at him and ran. "You'd better stay away, or I'll hurt you too."

"Okay, first…you're far from helpless. And from what I've seen over the past few days, I think you'd give anyone who tried to attack you a run for their money. You're very street smart." Mr. Stone grinned at her. "You should meet my wife. You and she would get along great."

"Thank you, I think. Who sent you to follow me?" She watched the other man, bigger than Mr. Stone, pull out a cell phone. "Is he calling for back up?"

"Something like that. How did you make us? I mean, I've been following you for a couple of days now and you never—"

"Four days. You've been following me for four days. Ever since I left the hospital." She put away the perfume, deciding he wasn't going to hurt her. "You've not answered my question, Mr. Stone. Who sent you?"

"You're not going to be very happy about the answer, but I figure it's payback for the mace. Mrs. Hunter and Daniel. Daniel and I went to school together, and when he called me to…where are you going now?" He walked beside her and grinned again. The man had a lethal grin, and she wondered if his wife was immune to his charm. She had no doubt he had tons of it and knew just how to use it. Much like Jesse did.

At the oddest moment, she'd think about the kiss. She'd not planned on calling it that, but after the thousandth time it popped into her head, she began to think of it as just that. The kiss. She stopped suddenly, and Mr. James ran into her from behind. She stepped away from them both.

"Does this have anything to do with the hospital bill? Jes… Mr. Hunter told me if I stayed until released that it would be covered." She poked Mr. Stone in the chest, suddenly angry. "If he thinks I can afford to pay that stupid bill, he's nuts. And besides, he owes me for that kiss."

"He kissed you?" The woman coming up behind them had her reach for the perfume again, but Jared stopped her with a declaration that it was his wife. "Wow, Jesse kissed a woman, and she's not falling over herself to have sex with him? I need to shake your hand. I've never met anyone that turned down the famously fab Jesse."

"Behave, Willow, or I'll tell your dad on you," the man growled at her. "Joey Foster, I'd like you to meet my wife, Willow Stone. Willow, this is the lady that Danny asked us to keep tabs on."

"What happened to your face? And what is that smell? Did you step in something? Christ, that's nasty." Willow Stone looked like her name. Long and strong, and Joey liked her right away. "Did someone mace you?"

"I did it. And it was perfume, not mace. Though I'm inclined to believe that mace might smell better. The lady next door to me gave it to me when we were evicted. She said she wanted me to remember her. I do, and don't care for the memory." Shaking her head, she started off again. "I'm going to see the Hunters. They have no right to have someone follow me for a bill I can't afford. Stupid people going around having innocent people followed and can't keep their lips to themselves. What was I supposed to do? Let him paw me right there against the wall? No, I will not. There was a perfectly good bed, not five feet—" She stopped again, and, this time, she was bumped by Willow. She looked at the woman and couldn't think what to say. She looked for the men who'd been told to follow her and noticed they were gone. Then Joey looked back at Willow.

"I told them you'd be safe with me. Though I think they're only a block back. Alexander is my brother, and he and Jared only were watching over you." The girl stayed with her as Joey started forward again.

"I didn't mean what I said. I didn't want to use the bed for—"

"Yes, you did. And it's okay. Jesse is a great guy, and I've known him nearly all my life." Joey frowned as a thought popped in her head. Willow seemed to understand and answered her. "No, I never slept with him. None of the Hunter men. They were just friends I grew up with."

They were in front of the building by then. She hadn't realized she'd been so close, or anger made her walk faster. She looked up at the imposing building then back at Willow. "I really don't want anything to do with these people. I'm trying to get my life back together and these people..." She looked up at the building again. "These people are way out of my league."

"They're just people, Joey. Just like you and me. They put their pants on one leg at a time. Though you should watch Jesse do it after you get him into the bed of your choice to make sure." Joey flushed and felt the heat all the way to the top of her head. "Go in there, kid, and give 'em hell."

Before she knew it, she was inside the lobby of the imposing building, and security was coming at her. She didn't reach for her perfume this time, the guns at these guys' hips telling her that they'd mean business if she tried that stunt again. When the first guy was close, she gave him her most charming smile and hoped she didn't look like a deranged idiot.

"Hi. My name is Joey Foster. I'd like to have a word with

either Mrs. Annamarie Hunter or Mr. Daniel Hunter."

"Let me see if they can see you, miss. Have a seat, and this won't take a minute." She turned when the door opened and closed her eyes at who stood there.

"It's okay, Tom. I'll see her up." When Jesse wrapped his hand around her arm, she thought he was going to squeeze it off, but his touch was gentle. "Come on, Josephine, let me show you to my lair."

His whispered comment made her shiver, but she tried to pull away. He simply pulled her to him and then wrapped his hand around her waist. She was well and truly caught. Damn it, one of these days she'd learn to think before he acted. She only hoped that he was kidding about his lair.

"I'm here to talk...your mother and your brother. I'm here to talk to him...them. Could you please let me go?" He pulled her into the elevator with him and pushed the button. She grabbed the railing as it took off with a lurch. He leaned against the opposite wall and stared at her. Well, two could play this staring game.

Chapter 7

He simply looked at her. He wanted to make her squirm, but he was starting to feel a little uncomfortable himself. She didn't speak, didn't fidget, nor did she seem to be bothered in the least bit. When the elevator opened, she stood up and walked out ahead of him. He moved past her and bumped her slightly on his way to his office.

Jesse opened the door, and she walked in. There were two chairs in front of his desk and a long couch. She looked at the couch but went to one of the chairs instead. He was glad. If he had to sit next to her on the roomy furniture, he wasn't sure he'd be able to keep his hands off her. Sitting in his large chair behind the desk, he leaned back, hoping that soon she'd give in.

She was beautiful. Her hair was long and dark, and as it was loose about her shoulders, he could see that it was straight. Her eyes were a brilliant blue, much like the sea off the Caribbean he'd been to last month. She was tall but not overly thin, but he was sure that if she lived in a real home, she'd put on weight. He knew from touching her she had full, heavy breasts, and her nipples were as thick as his thumb. Shifting on his seat, he continued to stare at her. She still

61

hadn't spoken a word.

About ten minutes into their contest of wills, she yawned. She didn't even try to stifle it, but opened her mouth hugely and then sighed when she finished. He had to work hard at not joining her, even after she did it four more times. He watched as she stretched, her body spilling out of the chair like a cat after a long nap. Jesse sat up and leaned against his desk, wondering if he could go turn the air conditioning lower because he was burning up.

When his phone rang, he leaped at it like a lifeline. He heard her giggle and felt his cock twitch in his pants. He hoped that whoever was on the phone needed him right fucking now. Because if he stayed much longer, he was going to try and take her again.

"Jesse, please see if you can get Joey to come to my office. The FBI would like to have a word or two with her."

He closed his eyes at his mother's request. This was not going to make Josephine happy at all.

"Tell her that she is free to speak to them about this."

He looked over at Josephine. She was glaring at him, and he knew that she'd heard his mother. He repeated it to her anyway.

"No." She stood up. "And if you're finished playing your little mind games, I'd like to leave. I have to find...I have things to do."

"Let me call you back," he said into the phone before hanging up. He came around his desk as Josephine went to the door. When he reached out to touch her, she turned quickly and put up her fists.

He might have laughed at her but was reasonably sure that she'd hurt him. And this time, she wouldn't stop at his nuts. He put up his hands in defense and took a step back. "May I ask you why you won't help us?" Her laugh didn't sound like she was amused, but he continued. "Mrs. Jennings, the real estate agent, may have committed a crime in that she took out some insurance policies on the buildings and could have started the fire herself. Her and probably her brother-in-law."

"And this affects me how? Or are you going to threaten me again if I don't cooperate? Why should I care if that woman goes to prison or wherever? You people have done nothing but make my life—" She turned away, and he knew she was crying.

"Josephine, I'm—"

"Stop calling me that," she snapped. "I'm Joey. Everyone, with the exception of you, calls me that. Why are you so stubborn?"

He wanted to point out that he thought she might be a tad bit more stubborn but didn't. He continued with trying to get her to help with the Feds. He put his hands down but didn't reach for her. "Look. Come and talk to them. If they don't need anything from you, then you can go. I mean it. And I'll even help you find some employment if you want."

"I don't need your help. I have a perfectly good job." She stood there and didn't move. He didn't either. Waiting for her to make a decision was the hardest thing he'd done in a while. "I can leave if they piss me off?"

He nodded. "Yes. I'll even be there for you if you'd like. That way, you'll have representation if you…if you happen to try to kick them."

"I thought you were just in charge of security and stuff like that." She sounded nervous, and he laughed a little at her tone. She made it sound as if he didn't do all that much.

"I have a law degree like all my brothers do. My mom wanted us to stay on the straight and narrow and figured the best way to ensure that was to know the laws before we broke them. I have a small practice outside of security."

"Small?" she snorted. "Probably in a building as big as this one with two hundred clients. I just wanted to go to college, but something kept coming up. Then you guys took my home and the homes of a lot of other people."

"I didn't...we didn't know. There's more to that than you were told. Besides," he said as they moved down the hall. "If we hadn't needed your building, we wouldn't have met." He'd tried for a joke, but he could see it had failed. When she nodded, he motioned which way for her to go, and she walked beside him. She asked to go to the bathroom, and he showed her to the one in the hall across from his mother's office. As she went into the small room, he knocked on the door to his mom's office. "She's going to help, but she's not happy about it. And she said if they piss her off, she'll leave anyway." He looked over at the two men sitting at the table when one of them cleared his throat. "I promised her, Mom. I owe her."

"Of course. I'll help you."

Josephine came out of the bathroom and stood in the hall. She glanced at the elevator several times, and he was sure she was going to bolt. But true to her word, she went into the spacious office.

~~~

Joey sat at the table as indicated by one of the suits. She'd never been interviewed by the FBI before and hoped never to have the experience again. The man across from her introduced her to all the people in the room.

"I'm Agent Alan Levy; this is my partner Agent Louie Velasquez. Now then. Miss Foster, I'm going to send the others out and then we'll—"

"No." She didn't say anything. She waited for him to tell her that he was in charge, and she would simply get up and leave. Instead, one of the Hunters, she thought his name was Daniel, spoke.

"Miss Foster, whatever you say needs to be said to these gentlemen without us being in the room because he wants to verify the story. If we stay then—"

"You weren't there. None of you were there, and the time that Mrs. Hunter was, she was out cold. No. If they don't stay, then neither do I." She glanced at Jesse to see if he would do as he said, but wasn't able to read his face. She thought he looked like he was going to explode with laughter.

"Miss Foster, I don't think you understand the gravity of the situation. There have been major—"

"I don't think *you* understand, Mr. Levy. I don't want to be here, and the only way I'm staying is if they do. I don't want anyone coming to me later and saying that I said this or that. You do this my way, or I'm booking it."

"We could have you arrested for obstruction of justice, Miss Foster. This is a serious crime, and with it, there are serious consequences."

She stood up to leave.

"You win," the other man, Velasquez, said. "Please have a seat, and we'll proceed your way. You're going to have to give us everything if we play by your rules, all right?" She nodded at Mr. Levy. "But you'll need to have a lawyer. I think I want to insist on that."

"I'm going to represent her." She watched Jesse sit next to her. She noticed that he'd removed his jacket. Holy hell, the man could fill out a shirt. She flushed when she realized he was staring at her as she ogled him, and she turned back to the agents.

"I was in my area, having just gotten off work when I smelled the smoke." She closed her eyes, knowing somehow this was going to come back and bite her in the ass. "I found the two ladies on the third floor. Mrs. Hunter was on the floor with a bloodied forehead, and the other woman was standing near the window. When I came in, the first thing she said was that the woman on the floor was dead. She said that she'd had a heart attack and that she would verify it if asked."

"How did you know Mrs. Jennings was not telling you the truth?"

She looked at the other agent. "You mean, how did I know she was lying? I didn't. Not until I checked her pulse. Then she told Mrs. Hunter that I had planned on leaving her. I hadn't."

"She did too," Mrs. Hunter interrupted her. "Joey told me that she'd had no intention of leaving me. She said that I'd probably prefer a sore head rather than a burned one. I agreed."

"What did Mrs. Jennings do then? Did she try to strangle you then?"

She looked over at Jesse, wondering how the agent found this out, and he shrugged. So much for helping her. "She tried the elevator. I explained that getting in, it if it worked, would be like being in an oven. About that time, another explosion went off. It knocked Mrs. Hunter sideways and out again." Joey closed her eyes, trying to remember what had happened next. "She told me that 'I'm getting the hell out of here. You two can burn the hell up for all I care. No commission check is worth getting my suit all smelly for.' And with that, she left us."

"Those were her exact words?" She looked over at Daniel when he asked. "You sound as if you knew exactly what she said."

"Yeah, well, I can do that. It's a trick, I guess. I can remember words like they're written in front of me. My grandmother used to make me recite books to her, and it came in handy." She felt embarrassed about her weirdness, and before they could ask her anything more about it, she continued with her tale. "I hurt my arm at some point, and my leg got a good burn when the last explosion went off. Mrs. Hunter was out again, and I had to drag her out. The other bit...woman wasn't around, so I took Mrs. Hunter to the sidewalk."

"You were right the first time, she's a bitch. I remember Joey asking Sondra for help. Several times. There was a verbal fight at some point, but I'm a little fuzzy on the details."

Joey was glad; she'd not been all that nice to the other woman. Joey glared at Jesse when he laughed. She just knew he'd figured it out. "I went back in. I could see the lady at the window. It was probably twenty feet or so from the exit. I thought maybe something was blocking her way. I didn't figure her to be waiting for me to come back for her." Joey looked at Mrs. Hunter before she finished. "I know this lady is your friend, so if you want to leave, I understand."

"No. You tell it. Tell me what she did when you went back in to save her sorry ass. And for the record, she wasn't my friend, but a realtor that we'd used occasionally."

Joey nodded. "I didn't see her at first. She wasn't near the windows, but when I turned to go back the other way she hit me with something. I fell forward and hit my head, but not hard enough to hurt all that badly. My arm was burning, and my leg felt as if someone was holding a poker at it. I tried to stand up, but she threw me back and straddled my chest. She kept screaming that..." Joey looked at Mrs. Hunter again. "I'm sorry, but she kept telling me if I'd just stayed out of her way, she'd be a millionaire. I couldn't talk, and I wasn't even sure what she was talking about. Then she said that had you died in the fire, she would have gotten double the payoff. She said it was a rider or something."

"It is a rider. It's a special circumstance policy that specifies that should you or someone else die as the result of an accident, the insurance company will pay double, sometimes as much as three times the policy's value." Jesse looked at Daniel as he continued his explanation. "If this is true, then this was premeditated."

"There's more, isn't there, Joey? What else happened in there?"

She stared at Royce and thought about what else had indeed happened in the burning building. "You have enough?" she asked the agents. Joey stood when they didn't answer. She was moving toward the door when Royce spoke again.

"She said if my mom couldn't die, then you had to, didn't she? She was trying to kill you so that the insurance company would have to pay regardless of who died."

Joey stood at the door with her hand on the handle. "The next explosion knocked her off me, and I fought to get up. I wanted to leave. She said that no one would miss a person...I staggered to the door, and she hit me again. I went down this time. By the time I came around, there were trucks and people all around Mrs. Hunter."

"Josephine, what did she call you?"

Joey didn't turn to answer Jesse. She wasn't going to tell him that she'd called her a worthless piece of shit. It wasn't because she didn't believe the woman, it was that she did. "I'd like to go now," she told them without turning around. "If you have any more questions, you can find me at Doyle's. I'm there most nights now."

She was at the elevator before the door opened again. She slipped in the doors as they were still opening and then pressed the button until the doors closed again. She didn't look to see who had come out, and since no one spoke, she had no idea who had. She didn't even slow down as she went past the security desk and tossed them the badge they'd handed her on the way through.

Chapter 8

Sondra wanted to go home. She'd been stuck in this same cheap, crappy hotel room for over a week, and she wanted out. Pacing the small room took less time than it did when she walked across her bedroom floor to her closet, which was probably bigger. She glared at the man lying on the bed, drinking a nasty-smelling beer. Clint Hampton was as handsome as he was a bastard.

"The least you could do is drink something that doesn't smell like your feet. I swear you are out to make this more difficult than it needs to be." She slapped at his foot when he raised it up at her. "And put something on. I'm sick of seeing you half-naked all the time."

"You didn't seem to have a problem with me being naked twenty minutes ago." She flushed at his bold statement. "In fact, if you want, I can take off a bit more of my clothes, and we can have another go at it."

"I fucking hate you," she told him. She watched him stroke his cock, which hardened beneath his hand. Her body responded to his; her nipples peaked, and her pussy moistened. "Stop that. You know that we don't have time for that."

"Take off your clothes. Right now, Sondra, or I'll do it for you." His voice when he spoke to her like that made her need spike. She didn't move, waited to see if he'd follow through.

When Clint stood up, he walked toward her, stalked if she was truthful about it. When he was less than a foot from her, he slapped her. Her head jerked around, and she whimpered. This time, when he commanded her to strip, she did so without hesitation. He was going to hurt her again, and she couldn't wait.

When she was standing before him naked, he grabbed a handful of her hair and jerked her to him. He was grinning, sadistic and mean. She could see his teeth and knew what they could do to her when he decided to bite her, what they made her feel. Before he could follow through on anything, a phone began to tweet at them. Clint tossed her away from him and went for the ringing phone while she picked herself up off the floor.

"Yeah," he said as he watched her. Motioning her with his crooking finger, he laid back on the bed and pointed to his cock. "Yeah, we got in last night. There was a mix up at the airport, and our plane was delayed coming out of Kennedy."

His wife, her sister. Dawn Hampton had no idea what sort of fun her husband liked to play during sex, and she didn't even suspect that he did it with her sister. Sondra went to the bed and knelt between his legs. At his nod, she unbuckled his belt and then undid his pants. His cock lay there hard as stone and uncovered by anything as mundane as boxers. As he continued to speak to her sister, she took him into her mouth.

His cock tasted of her from earlier. When he twisted her hair again in a tight grip, she looked up at him. His need showed in his face, and she could see the cords of his neck straining as he lifted his head to watch her. Moving his cock slowly to her mouth, he begged her to make him come now. Come now. She accepted the challenge and went to work.

Everything else faded around her. She could hear him speaking, but not the words. Cupping his balls in her hand and squeezing them tight, he surged into her waiting mouth. Before very many minutes passed, she heard the phone close.

"Ride me. Get the fuck up here and ride me. But you'd better not come, bitch, or I'll make you pay."

Aching in a way that was delicious to her, she did as he said. They'd been playing this game enough; she knew how to get herself off without him ever knowing.

Taking him inside of her, she rode him fast, hard, and without any thought to her own pleasure. Reaching behind her, she cupped his balls again and abused them as much as he was abusing her nipples. When he leaned up, took one into his mouth, and bit, she pinched his nuts hard enough to have him cry out in pain, and his cum shoots into her. He rolled them over and pounded into her hard as he came, each time hitting her clit in a way that had her wanting to beg him for release. But she knew if she did, he'd stop, jerk off, and leave her there. He dropped on top of her, his breath branding her breast like a hot poker; her body hummed with need. When he rolled to his back, leaving her lay there, he looked at her.

"Come. Do it. Come."

There wasn't a buildup of her release. She responded to him as if he'd been a puppet master, and he held the strings. Her climax ripped from her, and her scream only served to make him smile bigger. As she convulsed over and over, he pulled her to him and kissed her, gently this time, then held her to him. She loved how he treated her afterward.

For five minutes, she savored him as hers. When he finally spoke, she leaned up on her hand and looked at him from his chest.

"That was Dawn. She wondered if I'd heard from you. Seems to think you might be in trouble with the Hunters."

"No trouble, right? You said you'd take care of that girl and, when you do, it'll be over. I don't know why they'd listen to some street person anyway over me. The stupid cunt messed everything up by coming by when she did." He laughed; she felt the rumble through his chest. "What are your plans for her anyway? You never said."

"And I won't. The less you know, the better." He moved her off him and stood up, adjusting his clothes as he continued. "I have to get home. The little woman is expecting me. What are you going to do for the time being?"

She had no idea. She couldn't go out, couldn't call anyone, and she certainly couldn't go to a better hotel. She shrugged at him. What could she say that he didn't already know? When he left, she took a shower and climbed back into the bed naked.

"Next week," she said out loud. "Next week, this will all be a bad dream. I'll be in the south of France enjoying my new house and having a good laugh about all this bullshit." Even as she rolled to her side, she wondered if it would be that quick. Clint tended to do things in his own time frame.

~~~

"There's somebody here to see you. Woman. Says her name is Will." Doyle snorted. "She don't look like any Will I ever saw."

Joey had been sitting at the little table in the bar's kitchen, looking through help wanted ads. Doyle had told her he'd bring in the paper for her when she'd left work last night. Going to the doorway, she looked out at the woman standing there. She wondered what she could want. As much as Joey liked this job, it wasn't really on the way to anything Mrs. Stone might have been headed to at noon on a Monday morning.

Mrs. Stone stuck out like a sore thumb. Even in her holey jeans and t-shirt, she looked nice, moneyed. Joey was sure the scarred bar, crooked chairs, and loud television were the only things that made the place look good. The bar was a dump, but she liked the people.

She walked into the main bar and noticed there were three people there having lunch. Wow, she thought sadly, they were really hopping now.

"Mrs. Stone," Joey said when the woman turned to her. "What can I do for you?"

"You can start by cutting the Mrs. Stone shit out. I'm pretty sure we're around the same age. And while I like my mother-in-law, we're nothing alike. It's Willow, or Wills, if you prefer." She nodded toward a booth. "Your boss said he owes you more breaks than he can cover so we can talk for a while."

Joey looked at her bear of a boss behind the bar.

"Don't be cutting me with your look. And don't be stopping your talk 'cause you think I need you. I can handle a few dirty dishes if need be. Besides, Scott here has a tab he needs to work a bit on."

Nodding, but not understanding, Joey followed Wills to the booth. Within seconds Tracy, one of the waitresses/bartenders, came to take their order. Setting down two glasses of water and telling them the soup and lunch specials, she took off again. She went right back to the bar to watch television. She'd forgotten her soaps were on.

The menu wasn't large, just one printed page. Burgers, subs, and chips or fries on the top, and then there were the specials listed for each day at the bottom. Today's special was chili cheese fries and a drink.

Joey had never been on this side of the dishes she washed nearly every day. She hadn't a clue if anything other than the few things were good. And only then because Doyle gave her one of them each night she worked. Except the chili. She wanted to be able to not breathe fire when she spoke, and she was reasonably sure that her guts would thank her for it later.

After they ordered, Wills sat back and smiled. "Jared said to tell you he had to throw away his clothes, and he's pretty sure he'll never get the smell out of his hair. Our two-year-old son thinks he smells pretty."

Joey flushed. "I called his office to ask after him. His secretary said he was off site. She sounded...out of sorts, so I left him a message." Actually, she'd sounded pissy about her wanting to leave a message at all, saying it was simply a shirt, but Joey didn't say that.

"Carol. We fired her. She was a fucking idiot. She filed things according to cost. Do you have any idea what kind of mess that is? Anyway, we have Elly now, and she's getting us back up to business." Wills laughed. "I would have quit by now, but she says it's a challenge to her. I hope so. I need some paperwork like yesterday."

Joey laughed with her. She looked around the room again, trying to figure out why the other woman had wanted to come here. She didn't think it was for the food. She hated not knowing and, while she normally didn't fidget, she was scared. "If you've come here because of what I did to your husband, I don't have any money. In fact, as of last week, I have nothing." She hated to admit that but wanted Wills to get to the point.

Tracy brought them more tea and the salads. Wills dug into hers like she'd not eaten in weeks. When she'd finished, she waved the waitress over for a second salad and more crackers. The woman ate like a drover.

"I've had you investigated," she said between bites. "And before you get your panties all jerked around, let me explain. Jesse called me and asked that I give you a job." Joey dropped her fork and flushed when two people turned to stare. Wills continued as if nothing had happened. "He said that whatever I normally pay my people, he'd cover the cost, plus I was to give you an extra two hundred a week and he'd pay that too. We pay weekly."

"Son of a bitch. What does he want in return for making me a part of your payroll? I suppose to be naked for him whenever he comes by to collect his fucking due?" Joey shoved her food away, suddenly not hungry. "I'm sorry. I know he's your friend."

"Not to worry. Eat," she said as she pushed the salad back at her. "I wasn't very happy with him either. In fact, I told him pretty much the same thing right before I threw him out of my work site. But then I had you looked into."

"I would have told you. I have nothing to hide." Joey played with her salad while she thought of what the stupid man had done. "I don't have a place to live still; my grandmother is a bitch and used up all the money my parents left me, and I work for a nice man who owns a dump."

The food arrived, and the salads were whisked away.

77

Wills was two bites into her sub before Joey could get hers picked up. She wondered how anyone could afford to feed this woman.

"I have a healthy appetite. You should see how much my husband puts away. I'm just lucky he's a good cook, or I'd be as big as a house." She took three more bites before she continued. "As I was saying, I had you investigated. And there is more to your life than what you said. You have an education that I need."

Joey frowned. "I have a high school diploma, which I'm sure you already have. But if you want it, it's yours."

Wills laughed and sat back, finished with her meal. With a wave of her hand, all the dishes were cleared away, and a rag to clean off the table was left behind. "No. I'm talking about the one you started in college, the landscaping architectural design one. Your professors said you had a natural talent." Wills reached for a folder and laid out a blueprint after giving the table a very thorough wipe down. "This is the building we're finishing up on. As you can see, the landscaping is all around the place. All but a few things are in the ground, but a lot of them are already dying. And I fired the last landscaper. He was an idiot, even I can see that."

Joey looked at the building and noticed immediately that there were windows all around the bottom half. Wills put several pictures next to where she'd pointed and told her that's what he'd done so far. Excitement rushed over Joey, but she didn't let it show. Instead, she leaned back as Wills had.

"There are too many spring flowers and nothing for the summer. I assume that the owner wants to be able to see the flowers year round."

Wills nodded.

"The bushes are going to be a lot of work to keep trimmed down because if you don't have someone there nearly daily, they'll outgrow the color and cover the windows up." She handed her back the pictures. "Why are you showing me this?"

Wills stood suddenly and dropped forty dollars on the table. She was rolling up the blueprints as she stood there, grinning. "You're coming with me. I want to see what you can do with the mess I have."

Joey looked at the bar. Doyle was grinning like a loon and pointing to the door. "You'd better get going, girl. She don't look like somebody that likes to be kept waiting."

Scrambling out of the booth, she darted toward the door. Doyle tossed her a bottle of water and her coat. With a quick thanks, she was out the door. But what was there had her stop dead in her tracks.

"Jared hates it when I drive. He said I'm a menace. I compromise when I can and take this thing. Get in." The limo driver nodded, tipped his hat at them both, and held the door while they both got in. "But what Jared doesn't know is that Thomas here has a heavier foot than me."

The driver winked at them from his position in the driver's seat. As soon as they pulled into traffic, even as light as it was, she knew that Wills was right. Soon they were pulling in front of a building that looked nearly finished.

There were several trucks in the lot, and the limo seemed vastly out of place. As soon as they got out of the beautiful black thing, four men walked toward them. One was who she knew to be Wills' handsome husband, an older man who had to be Mr. Stone's dad, and two men that looked like they probably lifted houses as a hobby.

"Joey, this is my father-in-law and sometimes part-time constructor worker J. R., and my foremen Conley and Sherman. Guys, this is Joey Foster. Joey is going to do the landscaping for us."

"I am not," Joey sputtered at the woman. "I don't know anything about landscaping like this." Wills walked away laughing, as did Conley and Sherman. Jared and J.R. stood watching Joey and smiling. "She's insane. I just met her for lunch, and she brings me here to do this?"

"Yeah. You might as well do it. She won't leave you alone until you do." Jared looked back toward his wife, and Joey felt a pang of pain run through her at seeing the love on his face for his wife. "She's tenacious when she sets her mind to something. Just tell us what you need, and Dad and I will get it for you."

She looked at the huge building and then back at the two men. "I've seen the plans and the pictures. I suppose I should measure the areas and find out what the budget is to see what I can do."

Mr. J.R. stared at her for several seconds, then threw back his head and laughed. He threw his beefy arm around her shoulder and pulled her in for a bear hug. Then he led her toward the building as he spoke. "Budgets. I like that in a woman who works for me." He laughed again. "Come on, girly, lets us get you some measurements."

Chapter 9

Jesse wandered around his new building, looking at what they'd accomplished. He'd been nervous about doing this, moving out from his parent building, the one that had started them all. But it was time. He'd done all he could for the security department for the Hunter Corporation, and he needed this.

It was an older building. Not at all like the one that he currently worked in. This one was by far bigger in that the area around it was expandable as well as the parking garage that was next to it. He'd had the renovators in the building for over six months now, and they assured him that in another month, he'd be able to move in. He looked up when his brother and Alexander pulled up in the lot.

"Christ, this is an ugly building," Daniel said as he got out. "You'd be better off letting some demolition crew come in and tear the sucker down and start over."

"Nah, he needs to simply buy a new building and rent this one to me. I think it has potential."

The three men shook hands and then moved toward the door. Jesse punched his brother's arm as they entered. "You're just jealous that I'm finally cutting the strings, and you're still hanging on. I needed this."

Of his brothers, he and Daniel were the closest. When he started bitching about his lack of work about a year ago, it had been Daniel that had suggested it was time to move on. Even his brother was making noises about moving out. Jesse hoped so. He wanted to have him move into the building with him and be partners in law together.

The tour took them over four hours. Alex pointed out something in nearly every nook and cranny that he could use if he were to get the building from him. He said his computer software business was growing much faster than he'd expected, and he needed the room.

"Why don't you buy it and let me have my building? I mean, man, you're as rich as Midas, and I know you have good credit." When Alex flushed, Jesse knew something was up. "Okay, spill it. We're all friends here."

"Nothing. I'm taking on a junior partner, and his mom likes the old stuff. She's not so comfortable in the new building we have, but... Then there's the fact that she and I are pregnant again."

After several hardy hugs, only guys as good of friends as them could do without killing each other or breaking a back; they got back to the partner. After Alex's last partner had been brutally murdered a few years back, he'd sworn off having that kind of thing happening again.

"It's Jack. He's already graduated from high school, and the kid has a natural knack for computers. Sometimes he can figure something out before me. Plus, well, he's calling me Pop. I can't resist having him around so other people can hear him say it."

When Alex had met his wife, Heather, she had a son. Jack

was a wonderful kid and had taken to Alex long before Alex had met his mom. The two of them had been through a lot together, and now it seemed they were closer than ever. Jesse was glad for his friend. Thoughts of Josephine being large with child popped in his head so quickly that he staggered from it.

"You okay?" Daniel asked. "Are you just realizing that you're taking on a big deal, and it's scary?"

The laughter in his brother's voice was forced, and he momentarily forgot about the image. "What are you saying? Are you saying that you don't think I can make it?" A little anger and a lot of fear of what he was doing crept into his voice. He shook his head before continuing. "I'm sorry. I am scared, but it'll be fine. I was thinking of something else."

They ended up at their favorite restaurant about an hour later than they'd planned. The staff knew them all, so it wasn't hard for them to get seated and, when their drinks were brought to them, they readily toasted each other's good fortune.

They talked for hours, catching up on their lives as though they hadn't been doing this for years. Daniel still hadn't confirmed that he was moving in. Alex nearly was begging by the end of dinner, and Jesse couldn't get the thought of Josephine out of his head, especially the thought of her large with his baby.

He liked her, he supposed, and he could still remember her taste on his tongue when he'd kissed her. As he went into his house after being dropped off by the limo, he wandered through his house, wondering what it would be like if he ever got married.

The house was furnished, but unlike his two brothers'

houses, this one lacked warmth. Royce's house was noisy and full of toys all over the place since little Lee had been born. There were noises at Curtis' house too, construction going on for their new baby. He supposed that was it. Alex having another baby, both his brothers settled, was why he thought about a child of his own. As he passed through the living room to his office, he saw the gifts he'd ordered for Christmas lying all over the place.

Christmas was a huge affair in his family. His mom still hid the gifts from "Santa" until the morning of. She told them until they told her they no longer believed, she'd buy like they did. No one wanted her to stop believing either, so they simply told her they thought Santa was the greatest thing ever. He smiled when he thought of the first year that Heather had joined the family. She'd been so overwhelmed that they'd felt sorry for her. But since then, she'd been right in the thick of things with his mom.

He went into his office, thinking he needed to get someone over to help him out in wrapping. He only had four months to go before Christmas. He was still laughing as he sat behind his desk.

After getting his computer opened up, he started on his emails. There were several from potential clients, two from his mother, and one from Wills. He opened that one first, ignoring the ones marked important from his family.

You're an ass.

It started off. He smiled. Wills had never held back when she thought running over you was much more fun.

I didn't hire the woman for you. You can get off my ass about it. She's too nice for the likes of you anyway.

Fuck. He'd asked Wills to give her a job so he would know

she could afford a place to live. He was still trying to figure out where she'd gone when she'd left the hospital, but that was proving to be nearly impossible. He continued reading his mail from Wills.

I just found out from the company lawyers that my building, which was nearly complete, is a bust. The asshole ran off with his secretary, and his wife is leaving him. How stupid do you have to be to leave with some tart when your wife has all the money? Anyway, want to buy a nearly finished building? Well, gotta go. Jared is making my fav dinner tonight, and then I'm going to pay him in a way that only locked doors can work in. By the way, your girlfriend is staying in an empty building, did you know that?

"Mother fuck," he said before he got up to pace. The stupid girl was going to get herself killed. Or raped. Or both. He wondered if Wills knew which one and decided that first thing tomorrow morning, he was going to go by the site and speak to her. Wills would know something, and he'd buy the fucking building if that's what it took to get her to talk. He wanted Josephine here right now so that he could explain a few things to her. And maybe talk her into not hurting him again if he took her to his bed.

His cock hurt when he finally answered all his mail and made it up to his room. He'd been hard all night and didn't want to jerk off because of some twit that had kneed him hard enough to make him tender for a few days. But he did stroke his cock thinking about her mouth. Christ, he thought, rolling over. This was stupid. He was going to call a few of his old girlfriends and see if one of them was willing to have some fun. As he closed his eyes, the image there was Josephine, and he knew he was not calling anyone.

~~~

85

It was six when she showed up armed with books, pads of paper, and pencils. Joey was going to make this work out for herself if it was the last thing she did. Asking if she could sit on the floor near one of the lower windows in the new building, she was brought a makeshift table of a board over some sawhorses. She had everything laid out and was going through the books she'd gotten from the library when Wills came into the room.

"Conley said you were in here. Finding everything all right?" She handed her a glass of tea and sat on one of the large, round rings that had wire around it. "I can have that crap pulled out today if you want. I have some extra time on my hands."

"I have some ideas on both sides of the building's front." She handed the drawings to Wills that had small pictures of the flowers she was talking about around the area. "They are low maintenance, as well as perennials. Mr. J.R. said that's what you needed for the long term, but I put in a few annuals so there would be lots of color right away."

Wills nodded. "I like it. What are you doing on the other side? I think J.R. said he'd told you it was sort of an employee break area. There are a few of the older trees there, and the other jerk said that he'd have to have them removed before he'd even look at the area. I think that was what pissed me off about the turd, his lack of nature loving."

"I was thinking." She handed her another drawing just as J.R. and Conley walked in. "Mr. J.R. said there was going to be a kiosk out there for water and snacks. What if we did that and expanded it to be a water fountain? It would be both cooling and soothing." Joey had been nervous about that part. It would mean more money, more than simply putting in a bunch of flowers and bushes. She started to reach for the drawing back when Wills handed it to J.R.

"What kind of fountain you have in mind? Not one of those mermaid-looking things with water spouting out of her tits?" J.R. flushed. "Sorry. Not used to you yet not being in the business. I tend to have better manners when new people are around."

Will snorted at the same time Conley did. "I've worked for you for nearly a dozen years, and you've never had manners around me," Wills said.

"That's because you haven't any around me either." J.R. handed the sheets off to Conley. "Go see what we need to do to make this happen. Might prove to get us a new buyer."

Conley walked away without a word, and J.R. pulled up another wire container to sit on. Joey knew this was going to be bad and started to gather up her things to go. It had been fun, and she'd learned a good deal from it. She started to stand when Wills told her to stay still.

"What the hell are you doing?"

Joey sat and stared at her.

"You have a date or something?"

"The building doesn't have a buyer, right?"

J.R. nodded with a frown.

"So I doubt very much you care if the place has pretty flowers or not. I know that money can be tight, even on a budget. It has to be worse when you don't have a buyer for the builder after putting this much into it."

"The building is paid for up to a point. The man who bailed on us will either pay up or else. But that's not the point. In order to attract a buyer, he has to see it. That's where you come in. And don't worry about money. I'm a very wealthy man, and this company is as well." J.R. took another drawing from the table and looked at it as he continued. "I want this building to be your masterpiece. You do what it takes and let me worry about the cost."

"Then I don't understand," she said as she laid down her things again. "Why are you here? This feels like...like a termination meeting. I mean, I know I really don't work for you, bu—"

"You work for us," Wills said quickly. "Why do you think I went to get you yesterday? You work for Stone Construction as of you coming on this lot yesterday."

"Did you think we were going to let you do all the work and not pay you? What kind of bastard did you think I was?" His laughter made her realize that he was kidding around, but she still got embarrassed. That made him laugh harder. "Look at that, Wills. A blushing woman. You should take a lesson or two from this one. Could be a lot of fun for my Jared." He stood up and stuck out his hand. "Congratulations, Joey, you're now a construction worker. And so's you know, you will be paid very well. I keep my employees happy, and they make me money. How the world rolls, you know."

Joey watched him leave the large room, and she looked at Wills. "What just happened here?"

"Nothing much. You have a job on your own merit. You're working for one of the most prestigious companies in the world, and you are doing something you seem to love." She looked back at the door. "But there is a problem. Jesse is in my office."

Her body went hot and cold. She didn't know what kind of problem that was for Wills, but she knew the guy was probably still mad at her. She looked at the door and wondered if someone would give her a ride out of town. Joey looked back at Wills when she laughed.

"He's here to ask me about you. He doesn't know you're here. I told him I'd go back to the trailer when I dealt with a few things. He was swearing and pacing my office when I left. He seems to have a bug up his ass about you."

"I kicked his balls up around his throat the other day. He was being...he was kissing me." She looked out the window at the four men pulling up the dead plants in the area she was trying to improve. The bushes were next, and they went along with the dead flowers into a waiting wheelbarrow. "He probably wants a pound of flesh from me."

Wills stood up and tossed her empty glass into a trash can. "Maybe. Or maybe he wants to take up where you stopped him. Jesse is a great guy. A little pushy at times, especially when it concerns people he cares about."

"He doesn't care about me. We can barely stand each other when we're in the same room." She jerked her hand from her lips when she realized she was doing that again. "I don't have any idea what he needs from you."

"Good idea. Go find out for me. In the meantime, I'm going to see about getting the upper floors finished so I can unload this white elephant." Wills was out the door before Joey could form an answer. "Oh, and by the way, from experience, if you make them stew too long, a kiss will usually shut them up."

Joey stared at the opening the woman had just left through. Kiss him? There was no way she was getting that close to him. He would be mad, and that was understandable. But kiss him again? No way. Joey found herself outside the trailer before she knew it. She was pacing outside the door when it suddenly opened, and there he stood. Christ, but the man could make a suit look good.

Before she could speak or even think about moving out of his reach, she found herself in the building, and the door shut behind her. She tried for the door, and he simply leaned against it and glared at her.

"Let me out. I don't know what you're doing here, but I want you to move out of my way so I can leave." She crossed her arms over her chest and glared back at him. "I don't have time for your childish behavior, Mr. Hunter. I have things I need to do."

"And you think I don't? I came here because I wanted to ask Wills about you. Last I heard you were living in another abandoned building. Are you that naïve or just stupid?"

She snapped. "I'm not any of your business, is what I am. Of all the arrogant, pigheaded men I've ever met, you take the cake. What gives you the right to ask anyone about me? Huh? I don't want you in my —"

"Too fucking bad. Because I want you." He was suddenly touching her. His body was flush with hers as he pressed her against him. When he turned them, her back hit the door, and his mouth was over hers.

Chapter 10

Jesse felt her moan as it moved up her chest. He swallowed it when it spilled from her lips. His. He wanted her and damned if he cared where they were when he claimed her. Cupping her ass, he stepped between her legs as he lifted her. When her ankles wrapped around his hips, Jesse rocked hard into her soft flesh.

Moving his mouth down her throat, he nipped at the pounding pulse he found there, licked the hot vein as it went beneath her shirt. He wanted to taste her, all of her, and it had to be now. Lifting his hands from her bottom, he worked his hands up her waist to just below her breast. Running his thumbs under the heavy bounty, he lifted his head and looked down at her. Christ almighty, if there was anything more beautiful, he didn't know what it could be.

Her mouth was swollen, and her eyes half-closed. But even then, he could see they were glazed with need. Her panting breath moved along his own lips, and he wanted to taste her again. But he wasn't going to take anything from her without her consent. "Josephine, I want you. Right now, against this wall, I want to bury my cock deep inside of you. I can't wait much longer, but if you say no, I'll step back and leave." She looked at him, confused. He couldn't blame her; he was, as well. Confused as to why this woman of all women affected him like this. "Tell me yes or no, baby. I need to know."

He rocked into her again and watched as her eyes fluttered closed. He said her name softly, and she looked up at him. There was something else there besides lust; he saw fear too. But when she nodded, all he could think of was she was his, and he could take her right now.

Lifting her shirt up and over her head, he looked down at her breasts in the white bra. Nothing skimpy or lacy, but a serviceable white bra that he found sexier than anything he'd ever known. Watching her face, he spread his hands at her ribs and worked his thumbs up under the material and over her nipples.

Her moan came out raggedly. Even as her eyes closed, this time, she opened them quickly. He knew his own need reflected back to her, and when he lifted the bra up over her breasts, he continued watching her as he leaned down to take one into his mouth. Paradise.

Her nipple was thick and long. He suckled just the tip as he tugged on the other one. When she rocked up and offered him more, he moved to the other, took as much of her as he could into his mouth, and still left a good deal out to touch. He'd never had such a big-breasted woman before and knew she was the most delicious.

She moved his tie out of her way and worked the buttons of his shirt open. When her hot hand touched his own nipple, he let go of her breast with a pop and took her mouth again. If they didn't get naked soon, he was going to come in his trousers.

"Please," she begged him when she had her hands over

his belt. "I can't get to you this way."

He helped her off his hips but didn't stop touching. Her waist was so tiny, hips so narrow. When he felt her hand down his pants, he stepped back and held his hand over hers. "You touch me now, and I'm going to come. I've thought about this for too long, and I'm on edge. I want to taste you, take your cum into my mouth, and feel you come down my throat."

Her smile was sinful. She used her other hand to trace the length of him still hidden beneath his boxers. "I could take you into my mouth first. I want to feel you come down my throat first. Might make you feel better."

He couldn't speak, but let her turn him around with his back against the door again. He nearly came anyway when she dropped to her knees before him, her breasts still bare and her nipples hard. Asking her to take off her bra for him took him three tries. When she removed it and tossed it behind her, he groaned.

His pants were around his thighs before he could think about much more than the fact that the woman before him looked good there. Jesse watched as she licked the stream of cum off the tip of his engorged cock and moaned. "Hurry. Or I'm going to lose my load all over your face." She wrapped her mouth over his cock, and he felt the world under his feet tilt in all sorts of directions.

He watched her. Wrapping his hands into her hair, he tried to slow her movements down and hurry her at the same time, but she seemed to be doing things her own way. When she cupped his balls and licked the length of him, his eyes rolled to the back of his head. He could only think that he wished he'd had this image last night, and he'd jerked off with it. Then today, his need wouldn't be so close to the edge.

He pumped into her soft mouth and felt her swallow as he touched the back of her throat. A moan, this one harsh, escaped as he begged her to do it again. He was going to come, and he couldn't have stopped it if he'd tried. Tightening his fingers in her hair, he exploded into her. Over and over he fucked her mouth, feeling his climax come from every part, every muscle, and cell of his body. Even as the last of his cum slid from him, he watched her lap at him. It was almost too painful now that he'd come, but it also felt like heaven to him. When he let her hair go, she leaned back on her feet and looked up at him. He simply stared at her, not knowing how to tell her how he felt right now. The knock on the door behind him startled them both.

"Hey. It's awful quiet in there. Have you killed each other?" Another pounding on the door from Conley made Jesse think that he was coming in soon.

"No." He had to clear his throat twice more before he thought the man could hear him. "No, we're fine. Just working something out."

Joey reached for her bra and shirt and started for the back of the trailer. Jesse was disappointed more than he could imagine. He'd wanted her. Wanted to finish what they'd started, but Conley was saying that he needed some papers off the desk. Jesse adjusted his clothes, just realizing that he was nearly completely undressed.

When Conley came in, he didn't say anything but went straight to the desk. Josephine came out of what he thought was a bathroom and looked like she'd fixed her hair. He'd been pulling on it very hard, but no one could tell. She stopped by the desk and looked at something with Conley. Jesse felt like he had been dismissed, and that pissed him off.

"Josephine, I need to speak to you. There are things left undone here, and I want some answers. Now." He felt stupid when both she and Conley raised their brows at him. "I demand that you come to my office with me right now, and we get this living and job situation worked out." Apparently, he had stupidity on his brain because he continued on his quest to be an idiot.

Without a word, Conley stood to leave. Josephine was right behind him. As Conley brushed by him, he was reasonably sure the man said *fool* but didn't know for sure. Josephine nearly snarled at him when he grabbed her arm.

"Don't touch me." He let her go so quickly that she stumbled. He nearly reached for her again when she backed off. "You don't treat me like I'm your possession, no matter how much I get your rocks off."

"So this is because I got off and you didn't? I offered to relieve you first, and you decided to suck me off —" The pain in his nose made him see stars. And when he felt something warm gush over his mouth, he knew she'd broken his nose.

"You bastard." She left the office as he dropped to the floor. His head hit the cabinet behind him, and just before he blacked out, he wondered if he could have handled that any more badly. Probably not.

~~~

The dirt was really dark, but she hardly noticed it. She was going to forget what had happened in the trailer earlier, even if it took the rest of her life. She was reasonably sure it would too. She threw another shovelful in the pile she was making and thought about the idiot she'd just had sex with.

Well, not had sex with so much as he'd gotten off, as he'd called it. She dipped the shovel in the dirt again and wondered

95

how hard it would be to bury one in his heart. If he had one.

Conley clearing his throat made her turn. He grinned at her. He'd not said a word to her after she'd come out of the trailer, but she knew he was upset. She didn't care if he was mad or not. Now she wondered aloud if he'd been sent to run her off the property.

"Nope. I did help Jesse into his limo a while ago. Seems he busted his head and his nose when he tripped up on something in the office, though. Shame. Poor guy will have to replace his suit. I sort of dropped him a couple of times when we were coming down the steps." He nodded to the truck. "I'm to take you to the greenhouse. Boss said to make sure you get what you need. Another truck is on the way to get the rock you said you'd need to build the fountain."

Joey thought she must have looked ridiculous, standing there with her mouth open. When Conley pushed her mouth closed, she felt her face heat up. She wasn't sure which surprised her more, that Conley had knocked Jesse on his ass, that she still had a job, or that they were going to put in her fountain. With his "come on," she dropped the shovel and climbed in the big truck.

"I wish I had learned to drive when I was younger." He looked over at her as they left the lot. "My grandmother wasn't into driving so she couldn't teach me, and, besides, there wasn't any money for a car, so I guess it didn't matter."

"You'll have to learn to drive soon. One of us might not be available to drive you where you need to go next time. I'm only going this time because I'm your muscle. To lift stuff, not beat the snot outta somebody for you." She looked over at him to see if he was kidding about the snot knocking comment. But he was smiling, so she let it go.

Besides, she didn't think that once she got the plants and things she needed, that driving again would be an issue. Doyle's was close enough to where she was currently staying, and she hoped with the money she'd make off this job, she'd have enough for a deposit on a more permanent place and a good job. Maybe if she did a really good job for them, they'd let her use them as a reference so she could get one working with some other company.

Patty's Petal's was a beautiful nursery and owned by Patty Melbourne, a local. Joey had had to come here and work for a few weeks during school for a project. She'd not had the money for the things she needed and traded off the items for free labor. She only hoped the owner was the same. She'd liked the woman.

Patty met them in the lot. Smiling, she grabbed up Conley in a bear of a hug and kissed him soundly on the mouth. She then turned to Joey. Her smile was infectious, and Joey found herself smiling right back.

"Got yourself a job with a good company, I see. You should have come to me first off if you was looking. I'd have lied my ass off about the Stone men just so you'd come work for me again. Ain't had another person working for me since that holds a candle." Patty hugged her tight then told them to come along.

Joey thought that once she was finished, she would come and talk with Patty. She was so excited about the prospect that she nearly forgot to be pissed at Jesse for a little while. But once she was in the greenhouse, she was able to push him away.

They'd told her to get what she needed and not to spare the cost. They wanted to make this building look good, so they could unload it quick. Not. Mr. J.R. told her that they needed to sell it, but it was a bad mark on their company to have an empty building sitting when the Stones had built it. So, armed with her list and counts, she walked the path of the flowers and told her what she needed.

The greenhouse was laid out in a grid and all by color. Joey had been in several greenhouses that laid them out according to type. Patty had told her that a person knew what color they wanted in foliage, but not necessarily what plants. She thought that she'd put it out there so that people could get help once they had a color in mind. It worked apparently because the place was hopping with people even on a Tuesday.

Since it was coming on fall, Joey had decided to add as much of the fall colors as she could now with a great deal of springs that would come up next year. Summer, too, as a matter of fact, and Patty told her that she had a lot of the end of year clearances on most of that list.

Daylilies of several colors were on her list, and all but one were in the clearance area. She was looking over the list when Patty offered her a deal. If she took everything there, she'd sell it to her for half that price. Looking at Conley and his small nod, she agreed. He told her he'd have to make a call to bring another truck. As he stepped away, Patty approached her about working part-time for her.

"Can't be too much need for you working for the Stones in the winter months, and I got a whole house to fill. I'll pay you too."

"I'm only helping them out on this one job. Wills, the owner's wife, sort of forced me into it. I'm going to need something more full-time when you can do it, though." Conley stepped toward them as she finished speaking, and he had an odd look on his face. "Are they thinking I shouldn't have bought this?"

He shook his head. "No. They're sending two more trucks, but I think you got it —" His phone ringing cut him off. He stepped away again and answered. When he came back, he was grinning. "Seems I'm needed back at the site. Wills is having problems with one of the boys, and somebody has to hold her back from beating the shit outta him. One of the others will bring you back."

He took off at a run toward his truck and only stopped long enough to hand something to one of the others that worked for Patty before spinning out of the lot. The boy, Tad by his name tag, handed Joey a credit card. "He said he was supposed to give this to you first and forgot." As he wandered away, Joey looked at Patty. She had a huge smile on her face.

"That's a gold card. Come on, let me help you make the sucker cringe a bit." Joey didn't know what she meant, but by the time she was finished, she thought maybe the sucker wasn't just cringing, but having a massive heart attack too. She only hoped that when they got the bill, they didn't make her pay it all back. Joey was hyperventilating by the time she pulled into the lot at the site four hours later.

And it was well past three in the morning when she staggered home after planting until she had to leave for the bar then help Doyle close down. She was sure that there were parts of her that didn't hurt right now, but she didn't know where that was. Exhausted and dirty, she took a very cold shower in the empty building then crawled into her sleeping bag. She was actually looking forward to more abuse like this in the morning.

Chapter 11

Jesse was waiting in her driveway when his mom got home. He needed to talk to her, and for reasons he couldn't begin to understand, wanted her to tell him that every name he called himself throughout the evening and all night weren't half as bad as he thought they should be. He'd been a total ass, and he knew it.

"Jesse Michael Hunter, what have you done now?" He raised a brow at her, and she continued. "I've had four calls today from your brothers telling me that you're sporting two black eyes and a busted lip. I can see now that they weren't kidding. Is that the reason you didn't stay all day at work?"

"Yes and no. Can we take this inside? I could use a drink, and you might want one too. At least you might need it to throw in my face." She looked hard at him, and he let her. He was sure she could see what he'd been feeling all day.

They went to the den and sat down. The cook, Lucy Mae, took one look at them, shooed off the maid, and took the tray of crackers in cheese into the room with them. As she made sure they were all served with drinks and food, she turned to him. "This girl, you hurt her like she hurt you?" He winced at the direct question and shook his head. "Good for you. And

101

her. She needed a reason to hit you like she did, I'm guessing?"

"Yes, ma'am. I was an ass. Probably more than that, but in mixed company, I'll leave it at that."

Lucy looked over at his mom. "You gonna beat his bottom like I told you to do more'n one occasion when he was a boy?"

Jesse looked at his mom as she stared at him again. "No. I think he's doing that all by himself." She looked up at her and knew that the two women had always been more than simply cook and employer; they were friends. "Lucy, could you add another plate to the table for us? And we might be a bit. Will that be a problem with dinner?"

Lucy snorted indelicately. "No. You ever have a bad dinner from here? I don't think so. You mind your son, and I'll mind my dinner."

They both watched her as she huffed from the room. She was still muttering about dinners and bad boys as she closed the door behind her. Jesse turned back to his mom and apologized.

"I don't think you should be doing that to me, but I think I understand. Who is she?"

"Josephine Foster." He got up to get more ice in her glass and paced the room as he continued. "I was stupid. More than that, I was hurtful to her. I never touched her, but—"

"I know that, son. I know you well enough to know that you'd never hit. But she was mad enough at you to hurt you. What happened, and don't leave anything out. I'm not so old or stupid as to think that my sons aren't having sex."

He nodded, knowing now why he'd come here. He and his mom had always had a great relationship. He'd been able to speak to her about anything and everything. Unlike his brothers, he wasn't afraid to tell her when he'd fucked up.

And use that verbiage to tell her so.

"I should have taken her home. At least somewhere to make sure she wasn't as needy as I'd been. But I was embarrassed at the way she'd dismissed me. As if she did that sort of thing all the time."

"But you embarrassed her, too, didn't you?"

He frowned at his mom, trying to think how, when she answered her own question.

"When Conley came to the door, what did you say to him? Did you tell him to go away, that you had unfinished business to take care of? Or did you cover up what the two of you had been doing in there in the first place? I'm sure he knew before he knocked. You said you'd...err...finished."

He sat down hard. Had they heard them? Probably. If he thought about it, he'd never even tried to be quiet about his release. He glanced at his mother, who was blushing. He felt his own face heat up at what they'd been talking about. "She probably thought that I was trying to hide the fact that we'd just had mind-blowing sex. Or at least I had." He got up to pace again. "I didn't even give her a chance to explain either, but got pissy about her trying to ignore me."

"Well, that's nothing I want to know about, honestly. The mind-blowing part. What I want to know is what you're planning to do about it. I guess you are right. Or do you not care about her enough to want to fix this?"

He stopped pacing. That was where he was having his biggest concerns. Not only did he want to fix this, but he needed to. "I've only known her for a few weeks. Three actually, and I can't seem to find a way to stop thinking about her. I thought at first, it was because she saved your life, but that's not it. Though I do thank her for that, but I—"

"Have you told her that? That you thank her for saving me? I know that Royce did, as well as Kasey. Joey, of course, brushed it off, but I know they did offer her anything that she wanted. Curtis and Kylie offered to name their baby after her, and she told them that that was a horrible thing to do. Even Daniel has gone to her twice. She isn't happy with him, of course, but he did offer to go after her grandmother and get her money returned. The old woman won the lotto a few years back and is living off it." His mom stood up as she continued and went to the small desk near the windows. "And this is from the governor. He said she didn't show when he asked to have her picture taken for being a hero. He thought her ungrateful. Of course, I didn't tell the pompous ass that she didn't do it for him."

It was a framed certificate that named her honorary city employee. He looked up at his mother. "Honorary city worker? That's bullshit. Why didn't he give her a real job?"

"You mean like you arranged for her?" He flushed again. "What do you really want from this girl, Jesse? Sex? If so, then there are any number of girls that would give you that. Do you feel like she owes you or you her? I would think that you would feel that you're both even on that, wouldn't you? My advice to you is this."

He waited for her to continue. When she didn't, he knew she was waiting on him to ask, so he did. "I would like your advice. That's why I'm here. I like her. I don't know why, but I do. We've done nothing but fight since...well, I mean, we've done more than fight, but you know what I mean."

"Yes, I do. Date her. Take her out. Woo her. You might find there is more to her than you first thought. I know I have found that to be true. She's something else and, well, I'm thinking I'd like her to be my friend."

"She's not all that happy with me right now. Neither is Wills. I'm pretty sure she knows where she's staying and won't tell me." He grinned a little. "I think Wills will dig a hole and bury me in it with concrete if I go by her site again."

"I bet she would too. Joey works for Stone Construction. The building that Wills is currently working on is for sale now, and Joey is doing the landscaping so they can unload it." His mom stood up and moved to the door. "I don't think you'll be staying for dinner, after all, son. I think you should go buy you a new building for your new life, become a landlord to the James boy, and find yourself a decorator for the place you call home."

"I like my old building. And what do I want with a new one anyway? That one has charm."

"Yes, but you might soften up Willow if you buy that building from her, and that could go a long way to getting Joey on your side if you have an ally in your court." She stood in front of him and kissed his chin. "Now get out of here. And don't forget the flowers. Women love having flowers on their desk when they come in in the morning."

With that, she was gone, and he was left standing in the middle of her den alone. He looked up when Lucy came in with a list. He took it from her and, without a word, she left him. He looked down at the neatly printed list and threw back his head in laughter.

Step one, it read. *Tell the girl you're sorry every day for the rest of your life. Step two, take her out to dinner without sex. Women like that.* By the time he got to number twelve, he knew that Lucy was on the right path and pulled out his phone to make some calls.

"Hello, Jared. How much you want for that building on Hamilton?"

~~~

Joey was digging holes the next morning when she heard the trucks begin to pull in. It had been a rough night for her, and she was sure she was coming down with something. First, there was her boss yelling at her. Then there was the call from someone at the bar.

She'd put in another day like the one before, and Wills had yelled at her for over two hours. It might have been longer, but her husband had picked her up and put her in the truck to go home. Joey cried all the way to the bar.

Wills had thrown a fit because of her hands. Joey looked down at them now and could still feel the sting of the blisters that had burst. She'd been planting in the north garden when Wills had come to tell her she was springing for lunch. Joey had just wrapped her palms back up, and Wills had seen her.

"What the fuck? Did you even wear gloves?" Joey told her she had, but it was still nothing she'd been used to. "Come with me."

Joey thought about not following the pissed off woman but thought better of it. When this was finished, she'd need a reference if the job with Patty didn't work out. So with heavy feet, she went into the trailer where not only Wills was, but her mother too. Both women had cleaned the open sores and yelled at her for several minutes before they got a look at her shoes. For some reason, Wills seemed more pissed about her ratty tennis shoes than the sore hands.

"Your feet will have to carry you wherever you go. Those will heal," she said about her hands. "But, your feet get sore, and you're no good to me."

Joey took it, sat there with a heavy heart and sore hands, and let her scream and yell. When Wills stepped outside for a minute, her mom patted her on the hand and smiled.

"She's mad at me. I told her today that I thought she was pregnant, and she'd wanted to surprise us at Thanksgiving with the news." Mrs. James handed her a bottle of open water. "If she didn't like you, she wouldn't yell. Strange as that sounds, it's the truth. You should hear her with her brother."

After that, Wills had made it a point to come and check on her every half hour. By the time Jared carried her off, Joey was ready to murder the woman, damn the references. Then the call came at the bar.

"You think you can hide from me, but I know where you are. The empty building on Maple won't be standing much longer, and you'll be dust before they find your body under it."

To say she'd been terrified would have been an understatement. It had taken her twenty minutes to calm herself down, and all night, every time the phone rang, she'd been sure it was that person again. Someone calling her at the bar wasn't unusual, but that type of call had her sleeping in a different building last night, and she'd not gone to get her blankets.

Looking around the area, she was pleased. The fountain on the other side of the building was going to be completed today if the concrete was cured enough. The water would be turned on Friday. She reached down to get the next bucket of Canterbury bells.

These were the middle flowers in the bed. The flowers were tall, and the rest of the bed would fan out from them on either side. The purple of the flowers would blend well with the other flowers, poppies, and lupins. Then in the front of them, she'd planted petunias and bellflowers to hug the ground.

Along the wall where the windows had stopped, she had planted tall grasses. Oriental fountain grass was going to be beautiful from May until the last frost, and the Japanese eulia grass was going to bring the fall colors all together with its brilliant orange color. In the front of this, she'd planted hosta and Aphrodite, another type of flower-bearing perennial that was sure to blend well into the years with little work.

Joey was putting the last of the second row on both sides when she heard her name called. Looking up, she saw Kasey, Royce's wife, and Annamarie. Groaning, she told them she was nearly finished and would be there in a few minutes, but the women came toward her, talking a mile a minute about what she'd done.

The concrete for the walkways had been deemed ready yesterday, so all the barriers were gone. The woman walked along them in much the way that Joey had thought the employees would, admiring the color and the smells. She couldn't wait to go and work on the last part of this project, the fountain. All she needed to do there was hang the baskets from the hooks she'd had installed before the walls had been set in place. Two weeks and she was nearly finished.

When she looked up again, Jesse and Mr. J.R. were coming around the building. She'd not seen the younger man in nearly a week. She'd not forgotten that she'd hurt him, or him her. Ignoring the women and the flowers, he came straight toward her.

"Hello, Josephine. How are you?" He was close enough to her that she could see the light bruising around his eyes still. She flushed when she remembered what she'd done to him prior to giving him the black eyes.

"Fine. You?" She kept digging the hole that was going to be too big until he put his hand on hers. "What do you want?"

"I wanted to know if you'd have dinner with me tonight. All of us, actually. I have an announcement to make, and I wanted you to be there." He looked back at his family when she did. "My brothers are going to join us, as well as Kylie. She's coming in off assignment tonight, so this will be perfect."

"Then why do you want me there? It's not as if I know any of them, and I can't imagine what your announcement would have to do with me." She tried to pull her hand away, but he gripped her tightly, then stepped closer. "Mr. Hunter, I don't—"

"Josephine, you've had my cock in your mouth, and I've tasted paradise sucking on your nipples. Please call me Jesse." Her body reacted to his softly spoken words as though he'd touched her again. "Please look at me."

She did and was surprised to see humor there. She nearly snapped at him and remembered his family was very close to them. She took a step back and nearly tripped in the deep hole she'd been working on. His wrapping his hand around her and bringing her to his body was the only thing that stopped her from tumbling.

"You should let me go. I'm all dirty." She didn't recognize her own voice; it was deep and husky-sounding. "Please, just let me go."

"Say it, Josephine. Say my name. I want to hear you say it before I kiss you again."

She wasn't sure why he thought he was going to kiss her or why, for that matter, but her body didn't seem to want to listen to her head. Before she could think of all the reasons why she shouldn't, she nodded and said his name.

"Thank goodness," he said just as softly before he bent and took her mouth in the softest kiss she'd ever had.

His mouth brushed against hers once then again before he took her lower lip into his mouth and nibbled. Her entire body must have been connected to that area because she felt as if he'd touched her everywhere. His muttered, "let me in" had her open beneath his mouth, and his tongue swirled around and against her own.

When he stepped back without releasing her, she whimpered. And felt silly when he laughed. She glared up at him only to have him kiss her nose and take another step back.

"Kasey and Mom are going shopping first. They want you to go with them. Wills said you were nearly finished here, so it would be okay if you cut out a little early."

"I don't want to go shopping. And I am not nearly finished—" He kissed her mouth again, and she stopped talking for a second. "Stop that. What do you think you're doing? You can't go around kissing me like that. You're mad at me, remember?"

He kissed her again and pulled her away from the flower bed. "Am I? I didn't realize that. Maybe we should figure out a way for me to make it up to you some time. But for now, you need to go. Shopping, dinner, and then we talk."

As he moved away with Mr. J.R., Joey tried to think when she'd agreed to this. Before she could think of a plausible excuse, the two women had her in the bathroom in the building and in the awaiting car in no time. She looked down at how they were dressed and then at herself.

"What's this about? A charity shopping ambush? I don't really need anything, and I certainly can't afford whatever you ladies think I need. I have to budget my money, and shopping sprees with the rich and famous isn't going to help."

"Don't be silly. We're neither rich nor famous." Annamarie laughed. "Well, maybe a little, but dinner is going to be fun, and Jesse asked us to help you look prettier. We told him we'd do it."

Prettier? Joey thought she'd heard them wrong, but was too befuddled to ask them. Or she thought she wanted him to think she was pretty. She should have said no more firmly when they pulled up in front of the swankiest shop in all the state.

Chapter 12

Sondra laughed every time she thought of the story that Clint had told her about the call. He'd told her the girl had sounded terrified. Then when she'd gone to the building to see her to scare her a bit more, the girl didn't even have the nerve to show up. She looked out the hotel window again and wondered where Clint was. He was late, again.

Sondra thought it couldn't be but a few more days of this forced confinement. It had been three weeks since the fire, and, as far as she could see, no one had mentioned it in the paper for over a week. She was ready to resume her normal life and get back to selling real estate. She had marked a couple of obits in the paper over the week, wanting to get to the family before anyone else did. She so loved a good sale.

When she heard a car in front of her hotel room, she looked out again and suddenly dropped the curtain. The police again. This was the third time this week that they'd driven by this dump. Either someone had told on her, or the place was being watched because of the drugs and prostitutes that came and went like the night.

After a short time, she heard another vehicle come near her. She was about to check to see if it was the police again when she heard a key in the lock. Clint, thank goodness, was finally home. She ran to meet him at the door and stopped when he had someone with him. She tightened the belt on her robe and glared at the two men.

"Hello, bitch," he said. It was his usual greeting, but she didn't like it when he did it in front of anyone else. "This is my buddy from work. He's going to stay the night and then, in the morning, we're going to go and mess up our girl. He's going to help us."

They had discussed bringing in another person to help. Both of them had to lay low most of the time him because he had a wife and kid, her because she was wanted. The news had run endless pictures of her nightly until recently. Now it was just once a day. She felt both happy and pissed because she was no longer the lead story.

"Do you think that's a good idea? I mean, I don't know him. And how much is he expecting to get a cut of the money when we go back to work?" The slap knocked her across the room. Her body responded to it like a drug. When he stood over her, she looked over at the other man and watched as he took his belt off.

"Jon here is going to fuck you too. You got a problem with that?" Clint picked her up by her hair, and she went with him. It was either that, or he'd jerk until she was bald. "Take off that thing and get in the position."

She was already dripping wet from the hit, and when she'd had to get into their play position, she nearly came. She quickly took off the robe and stood before them both, naked before she got on the bed with her ass in the air. She braced herself for whatever came next.

She'd never had two men at once before. Clint had brought

women with him before for her to eat while he fucked her, or the other way around, but this was something new. They'd talked about it, of course, but he'd told her that he didn't want to share her with another man. She was glad for whatever reason he'd changed his mind.

When someone grabbed her hips from behind, she relaxed her ass muscles. She knew that Clint liked to fuck her ass when she wasn't ready for him, and when she screamed from the pain, he'd beat her ass until he came. She knew as soon as the cock touched her pussy that it was Jon and not Clint.

He was thicker than Clint, first off, and he gathered her cream and began rubbing it in her crack as he moved his cock head in and out of her pussy. Her head was jerked up again by her hair, and she looked to see a cock in her face. Clint this time. She took him into her mouth at the same time Jon slammed into her pussy.

"You like that, don't you? You're nearly all filled up with cock and can't come until I say so. *If* I say so." Her eyes rolled to the back of her head with his words. To be denied was the ultimate pleasure for her. He pumped harder into her mouth, and she held onto the mattress. Jon wasn't being gentle back there, and when he rammed something into her ass, she screamed around Clint's cock.

"You like my dildo? I asked Clint if I could bring it along, and he said you'd love it. It's thick like me, hard as stone too. But it can't come in you like I'm going to. I'm going to use this thing on that pretty pussy of yours while I fuck this tight ass." He pulled out then, and she was flipped to her back. Clint straddled her face and fucked her throat while Jon lifted her legs up over his shoulders and entered her ass.

She watched the two men. They were touching each other

and soon leaned in to kiss. Their tongues were winding around each other in an erotic dance that had her own climax rushing to the surface. When Jon reached down and cupped Clint's balls, she felt his cum jettison down the back of her throat while Jon continued to fuck her. As soon as Clint pulled out, he went to stand behind Jon, and she knew that he'd entered the other man's ass. The power of Jon's thrusts doubled, and she knew she wasn't going to be able to hold back. Jon moved down her chest and took her nipple in his mouth. As soon as he bit her, Clint told her to come.

She didn't come, she detonated. Her entire body screamed out her release, and it spilled from her lips. Even as Jon continued to bite her hard, she could feel his cum filling her ass and knew by the look on Clint's face that he too was coming. When Jon lifted his head, she saw her blood in his mouth and came again. Never had pain felt so overwhelming as it had just then. As the room started to darken, she wondered if Jon would want to play again.

When she woke, she was alone in the room. She didn't even bother trying to find a note. If he had wanted her to know where he was, he'd told her once, then he would have told her. When she stepped out of the shower, she heard the door open and then Clint yelling for her.

When she walked into the room, he was standing there covered in blood. Even his hair was covered in it. Startled, she didn't hear what he said until he drew back to hit her and said it again.

"I said I need you to find me some clothes. I don't want to get this shit all over the room."

Sondra hurried to do his bidding while he went to the bathroom. She wanted to ask what had happened but also knew this wouldn't get her anywhere. She put his clothes on the sink and went to the bedroom to dress.

He was naked and holding his clothes in his hand when he came into the room again. She sat still, waiting for his move. It was a game he loved to play. He'd give her something to see if she'd ask, then he'd beat her for asking. She was nearly ready to give in for herself when he spoke.

"Jon is dead."

And just like that, her mind took off in several directions at once. Did Clint kill him? He certainly was capable of it. And all that blood had come from somewhere. Was it because of what Clint had said, he didn't like to share? Then why bring him here in the first place? She looked up when he sat on the bed across from her fully dressed.

"Game's off."

She let out a long breath that she hadn't realized she was holding. Game's off meant they were no longer master and servant. She was his equal right now. "Why? Is it because of the sex or something else?" She stood to turn on the television, and he turned it off. "I don't want anyone to hear us. You know how thin these walls are."

"Yeah, but I've got a killer headache, and that doesn't help. Why did I kill him? Because you forced my hand on that one." She looked at him, wondering at what point she'd made him kill anyone. "You did when you came like you did. You've never come like that with just me."

Sondra didn't think she'd be able to explain how much she'd enjoyed watching him fuck another man, so she let it go until later. Instead, she asked what she thought was prudent. "You killed him away from here? Should I expect more charges to be filed against me in the near future?" Clint was a bit of a hothead, and, as far as she knew, this was the fourth or fifth person he'd killed in the past four months. He seemed to really get off on that. "I don't need any more heat right now. I want to go back to my old life when this one is over."

He didn't say anything, and she was glad. The last couple of times she'd brought it up, he'd told her that her old life was over. They knew too much and, when this thing ended, she'd have to go somewhere else for a long time. She could probably live with that so long as it was somewhere warm, and her sister wasn't nearby.

"He won't be found. Not anytime soon, anyway. He's served his purpose for what we need." He got up and pulled her into his arms. "I have to go home for a while. Couple of days at least. Clint Jr.'s birthday is tomorrow, and Dawn is making noises that I've been working too hard."

He kissed her pouting lips. She knew they were pouty because she'd worked on that pose for months before she felt she had it perfect. She didn't tell him not to go. She could see by the look on his face that he didn't want to.

He brought her in several bags of food and the small refrigerator and microwave he'd gotten her. Sondra wanted to throw a fit about it but was touched that he'd thought of her at the same time. When he left, she sat down and started making a list of the things she was going to buy when this stupid thing was over, and she had money to spend again. The first thing on the list was something nice for Clint.

~~~

He was nervous. Jesse had never had a date where he was afraid she wouldn't show or worse yet, that she'd be unwilling to be with him. He glanced in the mirror again. He heard his brother laugh and turned to look at him.

"Sit down, will you? You're worse than a woman. You look nice, and so will she. Mom told me that she looked lovely and that you would be surprised." Daniel leaned back in the chair at the front lobby of the restaurant.

"I'll be happy if she shows up in jeans and a t-shirt." But he did sit. "Where are the others? I thought I told them to be here at six."

"You did, and learn to tell time. It's only five forty-five now. Royce hasn't been on time anywhere since Lee was born, Curtis never was to begin with, and the only reason I'm here is because you bullied me into coming with you early."

That wasn't the only reason, but he didn't tell his brother. He wanted him here to drive him home if Josephine didn't come. He was planning to get drunk if she didn't show and needed him to carry his sorry ass up the stairs. Jesse looked at the door when it opened, and he sighed. It wasn't them.

"Why do women take so long to get ready?" Daniel asked him. "I mean, they do have a bit more to do, fix their hair up, make-up. I suppose they do have long, incredible legs to shave. I love a woman's legs."

Jesse did too. And he'd yet to see Josephine's. He wondered how long they were. He knew they were strong, but he'd not seen them naked yet. He'd seen her breasts and felt them in this mouth, but...

He had to stop thinking like that. He needed to woo her, his mother said.

"I want this to work out. I'm not sure why it's so important to me that it does, but..." He shrugged. "I need to see where it goes. Where she lets me take this."

He had thought about nothing else but Josephine for four days. Since he's left his mom's house and then bought the building from Jared's company. And at noon today, he and Alex had closed the deal on the older building. He leaned back in his seat and looked over at his brother.

"I want to start buying up some buildings around the area and fixing them up to reuse. Not like we do now, but as a rental property, not as Royce does." Daniel nodded but didn't say anything. "And I want you to help me do it. I know you have your hand in about everything, so will you help me out to get started?"

"Yes and no. I'll help you, but I think if we're going to be partners, we should be partners in that too." It took several seconds for what his brother was agreeing with to register in his mind. "And I want my name first. Hunter and Hunter sounds good to me."

Jesse nodded and shook his brother's hand. "Yeah, that sounds good to me too. Hunter and Hunter sounds damned good."

Neither man moved when the door opened again. The woman standing there took his breath away, and when Daniel started to rise to greet her, Jessed pushed him back down. "Mine," he told his brother as he moved toward his date.

"You're not happy, are you? Your mother said this dress was made for me. All I could think of is how much of me is showing. I have a wrap thingy, but it was too hot in the limo, and I'm pretty sure that she did that on pur—"

"Josephine," he said softly. And when she closed her mouth, he pulled her into his arms. "You look beautiful."

He'd not meant to kiss her like he did. He'd meant to only move his mouth over hers and pull back. But the moment he tasted her, all the reasons why he wasn't going to kiss her like he wanted flew out the window. The tapping at his shoulder was the only thing that made him pull back a bit.

"Down, boy," Royce said to him. "We're in public, and that, my friend, will get you arrested. Besides, Mom looks like she wants to slap you nutty."

Jesse pulled back, but he didn't let her go. He wrapped his arm around her waist and nearly whimpered. Skin, warm and soft, met him. When he ran his fingers up her back, he knew that the entire back of the dress was open for him. He glanced behind her and moaned. This was going to be harder than he thought. He looked at his mom, knew that she'd done this to him, and he was going to make her pay.

As they were shown to the room he'd reserved, he got a look at the dress again. Yep, she was nearly naked. And the way it lay over her body made him think she was braless as well as pantiless. Christ, he was going to die. Glancing over at Kylie, he noticed that she was grinning too.

"You guys did this together, didn't you?" he whispered to her without letting go of Josephine.

"I'm sure I don't know what you're referring to. I only helped pick out her shoes. She had the dress by the time I got here. And just so you know, everyone is rooting for you."

Jesse kissed his sister-in-law on the cheek and waited for everyone to be seated before he nodded to the waitress. The girl knew her cue and brought in the glasses of champagne and served them.

"Everyone, I'd like you to be the first to know that I've bought a building and have a new partner. Daniel and I have decided to go into business together." They all congratulated them both, even though they knew that he and Daniel had been tossing around the idea for months. The building was a surprise, however.

"What did you end up buying? Not that ugly one on Seventh, did you? My God, why that thing hasn't been torn down by now is anyone's guess." His mom looked at Josephine to explain. "The thing looks like someone built it upside down. It gets larger and wider as it goes up. I wonder at times why the thing hasn't come down on itself from the weight."

He took Josephine's hand and kissed it. "I bought the one that she's working in. The building that the Stones built. He cut me a good deal, and I love the landscaping."

Dinner was a blur after that. He knew that his family wanted to ask, but they didn't. He didn't know himself why he couldn't seem to stop touching the woman next to him. And every time she leaned forward or turned her back to him to speak to someone, he had to run his fingers down her spine. By the time he was paying the check, Jesse wasn't sure he had enough blood in his body to walk to his car, much less try and let her go at the end of the evening. And where to let her go was another question.

When they were in the limo together and moving down the street, he moved across from her in the seats. He wanted her but wasn't sure she felt the same. He touched her knees and nearly groaned when she trembled beneath his touch.

"I don't want this evening to end. But I made myself a promise that I'd take this slow with you." He saw her nipples harden under the silky material. "Tell me where you live, and I'll take you there now. If you want. Otherwise…"

"Otherwise, what?" She opened her legs, and the dress fell between them. "Otherwise what?" she asked again.

"I want you. I want you so desperately that I could pull you onto my lap right now and take you." He moved his hands up her thighs and closed her legs. "But I don't want you in this car. I don't want to hurry through making love to you because someone might hear us. Come home with me. Tonight. Come home with me and let me show you a passion like you've never known."

She didn't answer him, and he didn't rush her. He wanted her to think this through. Because as far as he was concerned, if she entered his bedroom tonight, she was going to continue to do so until they both decided it was over. This wasn't just a one night stand for him, and he didn't want it to be for her either.

"Do you know what I am? Who I am?" She shook her head when he started to answer. "I don't mean Josephine Foster. I mean, what my past has been, what I am now?"

"You mean that you don't have as much money as me? Or is it that you don't have an address right now?" She nodded, and he slid to the edge of the seat. "I do. But what would you say if I told you I didn't care?"

She slid her fingers down his cheek and smiled sadly. "I know who you are, too, Jesse. I know your plans too. Your mother and Kasey told me. What we have tonight, and for as long as you want it, will be enough for me. I want you to know that up front."

He didn't know what to make of her statement and decided that he didn't care so long as she was willing to give it a try. And she was wrong if she thought she knew him. He wasn't even sure he knew himself anymore. Pulling her to him, he kissed her. He showed her in his kiss that he wanted her, needed her, and her response was more than he could have hoped for. When the limo came to a stop, he knew that for as long as he lived, this moment in time would be forever etched in his mind. The first time he brought a woman he really liked to his house.

Chapter 13

He led her into the house, and they went to the living room. After he showed her around the room, they walked toward what he said was the kitchen. She didn't have a clue what he'd shown her in the other room, but this one she would remember forever. This was the kitchen people dreamed of.

"I don't cook here much, but when I do, I have fun." She wandered around the room, touching things as he spoke to her from near the doorway. "I had this room done to my specs but didn't so much in the rest of the house. I love to cook. Do you?"

"Yes," she told him as she opened the huge double-wide refrigerator. "I don't get to very much, and my grandmother hated to cook. I would fix these nice meals only to have her turn her nose up at them."

"I have a housekeeper, but she doesn't cook for me. Once in a while, she'll use some of the leftovers from something I made to take to her house, but nothing for me. If I want a meal, I want to cook it." He moved around the large bar and toward the opposite end where she was. "I have a stocked pantry too and freezer too. If you want to have fun in here with me, I'd like that."

She wasn't sure if he meant cooking or something else and stopped moving away from him to turn back to where he was. Neither of them moved, and she found she had to hold onto the countertop while he unbuttoned his coat and tossed it on the chair at the little table.

"Are you hungry?" she asked him. He nodded as he took off his tie. "Are you going to fix something to eat?"

"Yes. But I'm pretty sure what I want isn't going to be finished for a while. At least not until morning." He unbuttoned the top three buttons of his shirt as she watched. "Come here, Josephine."

She wanted to run and leap at him but didn't want to let go of the counter. She was a puddle just waiting for a place to melt. He crooked his finger at her, and she moved toward him slowly.

"I'm not sure what you want from me." She knew that it was sex, but beyond that, she wasn't sure. "I don't know a lot about fancy sex like you might like. In fact, I don't know much about it at all. I've only had sex twice, and both times it was sort of a failure."

"I'm not sure what you mean by 'fancy,' but if you mean making love, then I have to disagree with you on the failure part. I very much enjoyed what you did to me." She felt her face heat up. "In fact, I'd very much like to return the favor to you. Right now."

She stopped moving, her feet seemingly frozen in place. She'd never had a man do what he was suggesting. The only time before Jesse that she'd had a cock in her mouth, the guy had come so fast she didn't realize he'd come until he pulled away and started getting dressed.

Jessed moved behind her and wrapped his arm around

her waist. His hot breath on her shoulder made her tilt her neck for him, and she groaned when he brought her to his body.

"You fit me. I love the way your body lines up with mine. When I enter you, I'll be able to suckle at your nipples while I move in and out of you." He kissed her neck again and spread his hands at her ribs. "But as lovely as this dress in on you, I want to see you without it. Tell me, Josephine, what do you have on under this? All night I've been trying to decide if you were naked or not."

His hands slid to her back and then under the material that covered her breasts. She hoped that he didn't expect her to answer him because she was pretty sure she wouldn't make any sense right now. His hands moved to her belly under the material, and when he opened his hands over her belly, she felt her breath catch. Who would have known her belly was so sensitive?

When he moved them up her ribs, kissing her neck as he went, she moaned when he cupped her breasts from beneath. His own moan vibrated against her throat as he brushed his thumbs over her nipples. When he moved her forward toward the table, she let him. Her body was on fire for him and at this point, knew that anything he did to her, she was going to come.

He turned her toward him when they got to the counter. He never took his eyes off hers as he pulled the untied top down over her breasts. When some of the material caught on her nipple, he leaned down, licked the cloth away, and then took a quick nip at her breast too.

"Please, Jesse. I need something. Anything." She didn't think he'd believe her if she told him she'd never had a climax

127

before or he'd wonder why. She wanted him to take her away before he found out. But he wasn't going to be rushed.

"Naked. Just as I thought you were." He let the dress pool at her feet before he stood back and looked at her. When she started to cover herself, he stayed her hands with his. "No. Not tonight. Not with me ever. I want to look my fill of you while we make love."

Joey leaned against the counter and let him look. She tried to squeeze her thighs together so he wouldn't notice that she was wet. When he touched her hips and pulled her to him again, she nearly cried out when he picked her up and sat her on the counter.

"I'm going to feast on you before I take you upstairs. Every time I come into this kitchen, I want to imagine you sitting just like this and me between your legs." He pulled a chair over from the table. "I'm going to eat you until you scream, love. Do you have a problem with that?"

No, her mind begged him. *But hurry.* All she could manage, however, was to shake her head. He smiled as he sat down.

He lifted her foot and kissed it gently. He put her leg over his shoulder and did the same to the other foot. Now she sat before him completely exposed. Even as he moved his eyes down her body, she felt her pussy soak the countertop under her.

Kissing his way up her thigh, he murmured things to her. Most of which she didn't understand, but then a lot of it she didn't believe. He said he loved her. There was no way he actually did, but she did think he needed to say that. She didn't know why, but if that's what he needed, she didn't want to stop him. The closer he got to her wet pussy, the wetter she got.

The first swipe of his tongue made her cry out. When he slid his fingers through her curls, she watched mesmerized while he licked them clean, moaning the entire time. When he leaned in again, she thought she was ready for him, but she wasn't. Using his fingers again, he opened her nether lips, pulled her clit into his mouth, and sucked.

The climax ripped her apart. She reached for something to hold onto and wrapped her hand into his hair. Nothing had prepared her for what he was doing to her. Her body seemed to have a mind of its own and was soon riding out a second then a third climax before he stood up.

"Christ, I need to be inside of you. Your taste, your smell, is driving me over the edge." He reached into his pocket and then pulled his pants off. When he opened the package that would protect them, both she started to get down. But he had other plans.

As soon as he was sheathed in the latex, he reached for her again. Before she could figure out what he was doing, he had her lying back on the table, and he was poised to enter her.

"I'm sorry, love. I wanted to do this more slowly, but I can't." He moved his cock over her tender flesh. "I'm so sorry."

He slid into her hard. Even though he'd been a little rough, she came. Crying out his name as he pounded into her, she offered him her breast. Taking as much as he could, she felt him touch a bundle of nerves deep inside of her, and she came again. This time she took him with her. He stiffened above her as he let go of her nipple and shouted out her name as he came. She'd never seen anything so beautiful in her life and doubted she'd ever forget this as long as she lived.

~~~

Jesse woke to an empty bed. He reached to where he'd left her after making love to her again, on the bed this time, and found a piece of paper instead of the woman he hoped to find there.

I had to go to work this morning. I really enjoyed last night and hope that you did too.

He could see where she'd scribbled out something, and he smiled when he saw what she'd written. "Stupid" had been crossed out several times.

I hope you don't mind, but I took one of your shirts and a pair of boxers. My dress isn't in very good shape.

She'd not signed her name, just a large J at the bottom. He reached for his bedside clock and was surprised to find it was after eleven-thirty. He groaned when he thought about going into work this late and turned on the water as he called his secretary.

"Your brother Royce is looking for you. And your mom has called here three times. She said you'd better be alright, or she was going to kill you anyway."

He laughed. "Tell her I'll talk to her later. And whatever Royce wants, tell him if it's not important, we'll talk about it tomorrow. Otherwise, he can call me later. Much later." He nearly hung up when she said something else. "What did you say?"

"A Mrs. Randles called. She said that she wants to talk to you about her granddaughter before you get yourself in too deep. She said that she wants you to call her today if possible."

He leaned back against the bathroom wall and tried to remember where the name came from. Then it hit him. She was Josephine's grandmother.

"She's didn't sound all that friendly. I hope if you get involved with her granddaughter, she's a bit friendlier than that old bat sounded."

He thought that he assured her that she was, but couldn't remember. As he shut down his phone, he wondered if this was what Royce had wanted. Taking a quick shower, he called his brother as soon as he was dressed. He wanted to find Josephine, needed to find her right now.

"Where are you right now? I have to see you. Joey's grandmother was in the office this morning, and she's spouting off shit that will make your hair white." Royce had answered on the first ring and didn't even say hello. Jesse knew it was bad.

"I'm coming in after I go get Josephine. She's at work. I don't think she should be out where that woman can find her." He decided to call Wills and have her and Jared pull her into the trailer until he got there. "Where is the woman now?"

"I don't know. I had security toss her ass out about an hour ago. Christ, you should hear how she's talking. To hear her, you'd think that Joey has slept with everything that moved and then some."

Jesse knew that he was only the second person she'd slept with. After they'd made love in the shower, she'd confessed that she didn't have a lot of experience, hadn't really enjoyed it until them. He caught himself smiling at what he'd done to her later that night and wondered if she was up for some more fun tonight. He was sure she was sore. He knew he'd used muscles last night he'd not used in a long while.

"It's not true. You have to believe me when I tell you that." He knew his brother wouldn't repeat what he was about to tell him, so he blurted it out quickly. "I'm about half in love with her, Royce, and I'm not sure what to do about it."

His brother laughed. "I would suggest you finish up being full in love with the girl and marry her. This thing is going to get ugly faster than you can imagine. Mrs. Randles seems to think the paper should know that her granddaughter is only out to get your money and then leave you like she did her."

"Call Kylie for me, will you? I have to call Wills and see if she'll pull the wagons in a circle around Josephine. I'm on my way there now. I should be there in about an hour."

He closed his phone again and decided his brother was right. He needed to get over the halfway point of his feelings for Josephine and tell her that he wanted her in his life forever. He smiled when he thought about changing how he did the asking and not the telling to her. She wasn't going to be happy, as it was, with him.

The flashing lights and the ambulance out front had him nearly leaping from the car before he'd come to a complete stop. He was running across the site when he heard his name. Turning toward the voice, he nearly crumpled to the ground when he saw Josephine in the back of the open ambulance and Wills talking to her. Jared rushed to him before he could get to them.

"She's fine. I swear it. Look at me, Jesse. If you go there now, she'll fall apart. I don't know how she's held on this long. But the police aren't finished with her yet."

"Why is she in the ambulance? Is she hurt?" When he didn't answer, he looked up at the man. "Jared? What's happened?"

"She's been shot, but not seriously. The bullet went through her leg and out. The police said if she'd been coming off the ladder instead of going up it, things might have been different. Someone shot at her three times before they stopped." He moved so that Jesse could see her. "She's calm for now, but they're afraid for her. When she falls apart, they think it'll be bad. She wasn't the only one standing there when the shots were fired. Patty Melbourne is dead."

Chapter 14

"We were talking about the plants I still wanted to get. There are two places where the flowers just didn't match up with the way I wanted them to. Patty was going to let me work for her when I finished here." She looked at Wills and smiled. "You fixed it so I could have a good job later."

"You have a job, love. Right here with Stone Construction. Tell the nice man here the rest so we can get you fixed up, all right?" Wills was being so nice to her that Joey nearly forgot the pain in her leg.

"I was putting the hook on the fountain she'd brought over to see if it would work. She thought it was too lightweight for the size of the basket. I think she is right. It'll sag in no time." Joey looked away as something walked in front of the ambulance. It was a body bag, and she had a sudden fright then started talking again. "I think maybe she was hurt first. I remember climbing up quickly to bring the hook down before I bent it, and I heard the first pop."

"Do you remember where it might have come from, Miss Foster? Did it sound like it came from behind or to the back of where you two were standing?"

She looked at the policeman. It took her several seconds

135

to remember that he'd been there the whole time since it happened. "Behind me. I remember thinking that it didn't sound like anything to do with the construction, more like one of those pop guns you see." He blurred for a second, and she closed her eyes. Hearing her name, she opened them again.

"You have to stay with me a little longer. Tell me what happened next." He looked around and nodded. She did as well, but couldn't see anything out of the ordinary.

"Patty was lying there when several pieces of the wall crumbled over my head. I couldn't think, so I tried to climb higher. I don't know what I was going to do when I got to the top, but then the next popping sounded, and I was hurt and falling." She closed her eyes as she continued. "I fell on her. I didn't mean to do that, but I couldn't seem to stop myself. Then I heard screaming. It took me a few seconds to realize it was me, but I couldn't seem to stop."

"Miss Foster, do you know who it was? Who might think they have a reason to want to shoot you or Mrs. Melbourne?"

She opened her eyes and looked at him, but he wouldn't stay focused. She heard him say her name several times, but she was shaking now and so cold. She thought she heard Jesse, but was suddenly hurting so badly that she couldn't grab onto his voice. The last thing she remembered was that she had lost a good friend.

When she woke up, she knew that she was in the hospital. She wasn't sure why, really, but she knew that something had happened. When she tried to make her mind wrap around it, she hurt, so she stopped trying. Hearing someone speak her name made her flinch away until she realized it was Jesse.

"I can turn the light on if you'd like. They said your head might hurt and that we should turn it on slowly for you at first."

She nodded then realized he couldn't see her in the dark and told him okay.

Even the small light that he'd turned on was almost too much. She closed her eyes tight against it and waited for it to get better. Jesse took her hand in his and squeezed it. She returned the gesture.

"How you feeling?" he asked her. "I can call for a nurse if you want something for pain. In fact, if you need something, I'd really love to get it for you. I need something to do to feel useful."

"No. I don't...I hurt, but I think it's okay." He kissed her on the cheek, and she felt tears burn her eyes. "It hurts to try and remember. I know that I was injured, but not how."

He was quiet, and she looked over at him. "They said that it would be better for you if you remembered on your own. I think that's a load of horse shit, but they have a degree in medicine, and I don't. What do you remember, baby?"

"We were looking at Sheppard's hooks for the fountain. She told me that...Patty had come by to bring the last of the flowers. There were hanging baskets to put up, and I'd forgotten to get something to hang them on." She closed her eyes against the sudden pain. "We had put one up. Conley had brought me a ladder, one of those kinds that has to be opened. I was on the second step when I heard something."

There'd been a popping sound. She'd not looked around very hard because there were always noises going on around the building. Drills were humming, music blaring, and even, on occasion, more often than she'd thought, yelling at each other. Patty yelled out that it was shots, and Joey still hadn't understood. When she saw Patty fall—

"She's dead. Patty is dead, isn't she?" Jesse nodded. "I wanted to get away. I didn't even try to save her; I was so afraid. Then when something hit my leg, I fell off the ladder and hit my...the next thing I knew, someone...I think it was Royce, was screaming at me to open my eyes. He'd...I think he covered up Patty with his suit coat, and he was shielding me with his body. Why would he do that?"

"He's a great person with a huge heart. Did you hear anything else, love? Anyone speaking before you and Patty were shot?" He held her hand while she tried to remember.

"No. Nothing." She closed her eyes and drifted away a little until she remembered something silly. "I was seeing things then. I thought I saw that weird bitch your mom knows. The one from the fire."

~~~

Jess sat there for several seconds. Sondra was there. He'd known that the woman was hiding out and with good reason, but to try and kill Josephine? He looked up when Royce and Kasey came in the door. Without saying a word, he walked to his brother and pulled him into a huge hug. Royce held him back, and it was a few minutes before they broke apart.

"She told me that you protected her. When you came upon the scene, she said you'd thrown your...Christ, I'm in love." Jesse sat down hard and took several deep breaths.

"I love you too, moron. And if you mean you love Joey, then, duh. Anyone with half a brain could see that. You always were a little slow." Royce pushed his head between his legs and held him there. "Stay put. You still look like death warmed over."

Jesse stayed. Not that he had much choice, but he did feel wobbly. He heard Kasey giggle and glared at the floor before speaking.

"Please don't be fooling around while I'm sitting like this. You've no idea what my mind is making up listening to you two." He pushed against Royce's hand. "Let me up, dickhead. I'm fine."

He heard Royce mumble something about him being ungrateful, but let it slide. He looked over at Josephine still sleeping and spoke to his brother and sister-in-law. "She remembers. I wanted to help her, but she did it on her own." He looked at Daniel and Curtis as they walked in. "She said she thought she saw Sondra there. She called her the weird bitch that mom knows, but —"

"I'll have you know that I know plenty of weird bitches. Which one are you referring to now?" They all stood up when their mother entered the room. After each of them kissed her, including Kasey and Kylie when she came in behind her, Jesse continued his update.

"She said she thought she imagined that woman from the fire. There was only you and Sondra there, so she must have meant her." Jesse paused when Josephine stirred slightly. "Why would she want to shoot her? She saved the woman's life."

"Because she knows too much." They all stared at Kylie when she spoke. "Think about it. You said yourself that Sondra told Joey that you were dead. You also said that she tried to kill her in the fire. I mean, remember what her throat looked like?"

Jesse shuddered. There were still faint bruises around her neck. Reaching out, he took Josephine's hand in his and nodded. "Okay. So she tries to kill off her in the hopes of what? Resuming her normal life? Come on, she can't be that stupid.

Why on earth would she even think that was a possibility?"

Agent Levy, the agent from their offices, walked in just as Jesse asked. He grinned and handed a file to him. As Jesse opened it up, he was struck first by the man's impeccable timing and the fact that he was now sharing information with them that he'd not wanted to before. Jesse asked him why the change of heart.

"I need her help. And I figure the best way to get it is to let you all in on what we know. For whatever her reason, your girlfriend is the key to catching the woman responsible. And it's not just the buildings that Miss Foster was in." Agent Levy took the last seat and looked around the room. "This room is bugged. And a few of my agents are acting as nurses and doctors. There is one on every shift. The doctor that you have looking after Miss Foster is the best we have."

"I can't afford that." Jesse looked at Josephine, as did the rest of the room when she spoke. "I worked at the construction site until the project that Wills had me do was finished. And now that Patty is…is gone. I don't have the money to pay even this hospital stay, much less a doctor who is the best."

Before Jesse could assure her that her bills were not going to be an issue and neither was her lack of a job, Agent Levy beat him to it. He laid several sheets of paper on the little table and pointed to them. "Those are full benefits for you. You help us get her or not, and we'll still pick up the tab. Without your help, so far, we'd have nothing. Had you not gone into that building to save perfect strangers, we'd still be looking into who was doing it and not why." He pulled out another sheaf of papers. "That's a guarantee that the insurance companies are willing to pay. If you can help them more by proving fraud, then you'll get a percentage of their savings. Could be a bundle. This" — he pulled out a folder and laid it next to the other sheets — "is a list of what we have versus what we think you can answer for us. Like I said, with or without your help, we'll pay your hospital bills."

"Why?"

Jesse frowned, as did Agent Levy. It was obvious that neither of them understood her question.

"Why do you need my help? Don't you have, like, all kinds of equipment to get her? Or am I going to be your bait?"

Jesse waited for the agent to deny the question. Waited for him to say, "No, we need you for something else." Anything else. But all he did was nod.

"No. Oh, hell, no. You are so not using her for bait." Jesse got up to pace, needing to work off his instant anger or end up in jail because he killed an agent of the FBI. "I forbid it."

Jesse heard Royce say, "Fuck," just as Josephine sat up in bed. He had about half a second to realize his mistake, but it wasn't long enough for him to backtrack. He wasn't sure that he would have, but it was a moot point now. She was pissed.

"You forbid it? You do. Well hunky dory for you, Mr. Hunter. I just don't know how little old me made it in this big, bad world without you telling me what I can and can't do." He didn't like her tone or what she was saying.

"Now Josephine — "

"Don't you dare 'now Josephine' me, you overgrown, pigheaded prick. I've been on my own longer than you've gone without a designer suit. You forbid — do you have any idea what it was like living with my grandmother, who told me every day what I could eat, who I could see? Too fucking long. And now you want to come in here and make demands on — get out of here. I mean it, get out, or I'll have...I'll have that man shoot you in your precious nuts."

"Now see here. You can't talk to him like that. He is in lo—"

"If you finish that sentence, I will have him shoot you too." Royce might have said more, but Kasey was covering his mouth with her hand. But Jesse wasn't finished yet, not nearly so.

"I don't think you're seeing this for what it could be," he snapped. "She's already shot and killed one person, and she won't stop at just her either if she can. Is this about the money? Is that why you're thinking you need to do this stupid thing? Then I can tell you right now that I have more than what they're offering you." Again, he knew he was saying it all wrong. "I love you, Josephine, and I need to care for you."

"You love me. I see, and you *need* to care for me because why, Jesse? I'm too stupid and too poor to make sound decisions on my own because there's money involved? Is that the opinion you have of me? That I'm some sort of...what? Gold-digger?" Her voice was too calm, and he felt pains in his heart. "I want you all to leave. I'm tired, and I just want to go to sleep."

She rolled over, and he watched his family leave the room. Agent Levy was gathering up his paperwork when Jesse started to sit near her bed.

"I don't want you here either. I want to be alone. Please just go home and leave me alone."

"Please don't do this. I might have said some really stupid things, but it's because I—"

"Go away. I'm begging you. Just go away." She turned off the light, plunging them into darkness. He moved to get his jacket and looked at her again. She looked stiff and uninviting.

He thought before either of them said something else they might not mean, he'd better leave. His mother was waiting in the hall for him.

"You didn't tell her before this that you loved her, did you?"

He shook his head.

"I didn't think so. So, in the heat of the moment, in front of your entire family, you not only tell her that you're doing this because you think she's a money-grubbing woman, you think that blurting out you love her is going to make her melt for you."

It wasn't a question, but he answered anyway. "No, ma'am. I'd only just figured out I loved her right before you guys came in. But you have to know I'm right."

She turned him around so that he faced Josephine's room. "And you being right is more important than what you made her feel like when you said it. Oh, Jesse. I'm not sure you can fix this one. I think she's stronger than all of us put together."

He felt her leave him. Heard the elevator door swish open then ding closed. There were others around him; nursing staff, doctors, and cleaning people, but he would swear that he'd never felt so alone in his life. His mother was right. Being right did not make him feel better about himself.

Chapter 15

Sondra was giddy. She'd watched the news on the hotel television and had the little boy in the next room get her a paper. The top story was how the local businesswoman, Patrice Patty's Petal's Melbourne, had been murdered. They didn't mention the bitch by name, but they said that another woman had been critically injured during the shooting and they were withholding details until next of kin could be notified.

She looked over at Clint and kicked him hard in the ribs. He'd pissed her off last night, and now he was as dead a Patty's Petal's. She doubted that as many people would mourn his death as it seemed they would Patty's Petal's, but then she was reasonably sure that Patty's Petal's didn't go to her boyfriend's house smelling like sex and her ex-husband. She kicked him again. Then said *Patty's Petal's* four more times. It was like a rhyme, and she had fun with it.

It hadn't taken much for her to kill Clint. She knew he always had a knife in his boot, and she knew that he had it razor sharp too. Smiling, she thought of the fact that she'd given him good head, the best she'd ever given to him, as she sliced the vein running along his upper thigh. When he'd flinched at the pain, she'd swallowed his cock and had him moaning again. When he was too weak to fight her, she'd stabbed him three times. Once in the dick and twice in the chest. Of course, she'd gone back afterward and cut his tiny weenie off him just because she could. It was harder, she realized, to stab his dick than it had been to plunge the knife in his chest. She liked his dick. Then she started rhyming Clintie Dickie over and over until the news came back on.

Sondra watched the weather. Yeah, yeah, it was going to get colder. Well, duh. It was wintertime, people. She giggled again when she thought of how ignorant people could be about winter. It was like someone had said to her once, "Christmas snuck right up on me." Really? How did that happen? It came on the twenty-fifth of December every year. People were idiots.

The next headline was about how a church was giving out blankets again this year. Her firm had done that once. She'd been in charge of the event that year and had bought the cheap blankets for four bucks each and charged the company eight. She'd gone to Vegas with that extra money and had a grand old time. She thought maybe that's where she'd met Clintie Dickie.

A commercial break made her angry, and she nearly threw her shoe at the thing. She didn't have another television to replace it with, and she'd already gone out once today. She looked at her purchases on the bed and thought she should get to wrapping Clintie Dickie up before he became stinky winky.

When the news came back on, she watched the footage of the building again. There really wasn't much to see, but she did see Annamarie there in the background and a body bag.

Leaning into the screen, she tried to see if that girl was there, Joey somebody, but all she could see was police and other crime scene personnel. She wanted to see blood, damn it, not yellow tape around it.

When the news finally went to another story, she continued to sit on the floor. Clintie Dickie had stained the floor, and now that he was gone, she'd have to clean it up on her own. Moving to where the man lay, she put her head on his back and closed her eyes. He was dead, of course, but she was lonely and needed to talk to someone.

"I did something very naughty today. After I shot Patty's Petal's and killed her, I went to the hospital. But I went to the wrong one. They were mean to me too." She thought about the woman who'd told her that she would have to leave, that no one by the name she was looking for was there. "I didn't know you had to have full names. And I was about to tell her that I'd shot the bitch, I should be able to see her when I saw a cop coming down the hall. I didn't like that."

The cop hadn't even looked her way, but she knew that could have been his trick to make her think it. And she was sure that the girl, Joey somebody, was in that hospital. Why would they take her all the way across town to one that Sondra didn't go to?

"I have to leave here soon too. I have to get back out on the market. Do you know how many houses I've missed being cooped up in here? At least thirty. I've been here for a month, and all that money is going to the new girl Jezebel."

Sondra knew her name wasn't Jezebel, but since she'd never bothered to learn her name, she called her what she thought she was. A jezebel just like that Joey somebody was. She rolled to her back, using Clint as a pillow.

147

"You should have brought more cash with you, dummy. I had to pick up things to wrap you up in, and you didn't have any cash. Not enough, anyway. I had to use my credit card." She remembered the small bit of fear she'd felt when the card had to be run through three times. "For a second there, I thought somebody had canceled it, but she said it was only a power surge or some bullshit. She probably made that up. I thought about killing her, but there were just too many witnesses." She giggled again, louder this time. "I wonder what she would have said if she'd known that she had a killer in her line. Probably would have crapped herself. I would have laughed my ass off if she had."

Sondra sat up on her knees and looked at the mess he'd made. Reaching for the plastic shower curtains she'd gotten, she opened them up. It was going to take at least two, she thought. He was a big man. She picked up his dick with the point of the knife and put it in the used wrapper the curtain had come in. She'd thought about putting it in his mouth, but decided he'd enjoy that too much and simply put it in his hand after she rolled him into the curtain.

Blood was everywhere. Not that she cared. It wasn't as if she was going to take him out and bury him in it. She was doing this so he wouldn't stink. She had no idea how long a body could go without smelling everything up, but she was sure it couldn't be very long. When she'd gotten him where she'd wanted him, she opened the tape and began wrapping the edges up and over him. Just as she'd thought, too big for just one.

After securing the tape over his chest and arms, she moved down his legs. They were covered pretty well, but she still had to get him covered. She was just getting the second curtain open when a car door slammed outside her room. She waited for several seconds, and when they didn't pound on her door, demanding that she come out with her hands in the air, she knew she was okay.

After nearly four hours of wrestling with the dead man, Sondra was covered in blood and sweat. She felt...sexy, she supposed. All covered in blood, hair, clothes, even her feet were red stained. She stood up and had to grab onto the dresser. She had a wave of dizziness wash over her so quickly it was hold on or fall. She tried to think if she'd eaten dinner or not when she realized she didn't remember eating breakfast or lunch either. Looking down at herself, she realized that to go out, she'd have to clean up. She headed to the small shower.

The streets were almost deserted this time of night, she realized. Sondra had looked at her watch before leaving the hotel and saw that it was well after midnight. Still, being alone didn't bother her so much anymore. She liked her own company.

There was a problem, though. She had very little money and what little there was had Clint's blood on it. She was standing next to an ATM when she realized she still had her card. They may have frozen her accounts, but they hadn't taken her card. Walking up to the machine, she put her card in and followed the instructions.

When it asked her to wait, she looked around. This wasn't the greatest neighborhood in the world, and she stepped closer to the light that shone down on her from the building. When the machine made a noise, she turned to it.

"Access denied. Any questions, please contact your local banker." She pushed the exit button only to have it repeat its previous message. It wouldn't give her card back to her. Stomping to the front of the bank, which was dark, she pounded on the door. "Hello? I need to talk to my local banker. And your retarded machine took my card and won't give it back." Cupping her hand over the glass, she tried to see if anyone was in there and couldn't. "Damn it, I want my card back. It's a gold card, and I want it back. You can't keep my card from me."

She huffed her way back to the ATM and was mad that someone else was there. She watched as the person put in their card, punched in their numbers, and was rewarded with a handful of cash. Sondra walked up behind the woman.

"Excuse me, the machine there took my card, and I think you have the money I was supposed to get." She smiled at the woman, who looked at her as if she had several heads. "If you'll just hand it over, I'll tell them in the morning about the mistake, and you'll probably be rewarded for helping me out."

"Fuck off. This is my money. I'm not giving you shit." The woman started back toward what Sondra assumed was her car. There wasn't any way she was leaving without her money, so she tried again.

"I said that's my money. I haven't eaten all day, and now that Clint can't go out and shop for me, I have to do it myself. So if you'll just—"

"I said to fuck off. You want money? Then I suggest you go find someone who gives a fuck. I don't." The woman turned her back to Sondra again, and that pissed her off.

Sondra hadn't realized she brought the knife with her that she'd killed Clint with until she had it in her hand. The first time she brought it down into the woman who'd stolen her money, she'd been surprised at how easily it slipped through her throat. By the time she'd stabbed the woman several times, she knew that she was enjoying herself too much. Falling off the now dead thief, Sondra took the woman's purse and left the area. She was all the way back to her hotel before she realized that she'd seen several flashing lights, not unlike those on a camera.

There hadn't been anyone around, she was sure of that. And if the dead woman had taken pictures...well, there wasn't any way she'd been able to do that. She'd killed her, and now she had money to eat with. She opened the wallet first then, finding nothing, began to look through the entire bag. Nothing. Finally, in a fit of rage, she dumped the contents on the bed and found that, somehow, the woman had stolen from her again.

Sondra gathered everything up. She was going back to teach the stupid woman a lesson. But it was no longer a woman lying dead; now there were blue and red lights, yellow tape, and more cops than she'd seen in her life. Hiding in the shadows, she watched them. One of them looked like he was putting something in a smallish bag, and Sondra knew it was a phone. She made her way back to the hotel, clutching the bag to her chest, wondering how the woman had betrayed her yet again.

"I don't like thieves, and I hate liars. She was both. How could she do that?" Sondra asked no one. "I have to find out who she told I did it."

~~~

"She won't let any of us in to talk to her. I tried to tell her it'll be better in the morning, but she just won't—"

"I'll talk to her." Jesse looked at Josephine's door then

151

back at the nurse. "Did she eat anything for dinner?"

"Not much. She was…well, after you all left, she was quiet for a bit, but then when Molly went in to check her vitals, she was sobbing. That new girl we hired suggested we give you a call. Won't do her much good to cry like she is."

Jesse wondered if the new girl was the agent, but didn't say anything.

"You going to go in?"

She'd made it sound like he was going behind enemy lines, and he might not make it out again. Actually, he thought that might be fitting. Going to the door after reassuring her that they'd be fine, he went to the door. He could hear her crying, and it hurt his heart.

The room was dark, but the light from the bathroom gave him just enough to see that Josephine was huddled in the bed. He cleared his throat when he started taking off his coat. This was going to be hard, he realized. Harder than his first case when he'd thrown up for over an hour before the session was called.

"What are you doing here? I thought I told you to go away. I don't want you around here anymore." Her voice sounded watery and hurt. He tried to ignore how much it hurt him to hear her throw him out again.

"The news said it was going to be beautiful tomorrow. I can't believe that. It's kinda cold out even for this time of year." Small talk. He should be good at that. "I'll have to pull out the winter suits if this keeps up."

"Well, bully for you. I bet you have a whole closet of winter suits, as well as every season there is. Am I going to have to call security to have your ass thrown out?"

"They work for me, so they won't do it. I do have a lot of

suits. I wonder why that is. I don't wear more than a dozen of them." He sat down to pull off his boots after removing both his coat and his suit jacket. "But shoes...I've never been a big shoe collector. My brother is. Curtis. I wonder how he explained to his wife why he had so many."

As his second boot hit the floor, he stood up and looked at her. She'd turned on the light now, the upper one, so she was cast in shadows. But he could see that she'd been crying and he hated it.

"How do they work for you? This is the hospital. You don't own this building too, do you? I wouldn't be...what are you doing now?" Her voice had lost its watery quality and was now squeaky with surprise.

He hid his face while he fussed with his belt. "I'm getting ready for bed. I don't know what to do with my wallet, do you?" She didn't answer, and he pulled his belt off and tossed it toward the chair. Pulling out his wallet, he put it under her pillow and watched her swallow three times as he tried to find the perfect place. "That should do it. Now, would you prefer me with our without my boxers?"

"You get dressed right now. I don't know what you're trying to pull, but you are not getting in this bed. I'm here, and, in case it escaped your notice, I'm hurt."

"Well, of course, you're hurt. If you weren't, we'd be at my house and in my bed. None of this trying to find a place to hide my wallet." He undid the top button of his pants and then started to unbutton his shirt. He'd long since taken his tie off before getting here tonight. "Plus, my bed is much bigger. And probably much softer." He pressed on the bed nearest her bottom and nodded. "Much."

"I said you had to...to leave here. Please don't...you...

you should…Jesse, don't do this." He stopped at midway on his shirt. "You have to leave here. You might get…what if that person comes here?"

Jesse finished getting his shirt off in record time and slipped out of his pants. Before she could move away from him, whether that was her intention or not, he got into the bed with her and pulled her into his arms. "No one is coming here, love. Not tonight. There are too many people out there to protect us." She was stiff in his arms, but he didn't let her go. "Did you know that my mother is worried about you? She told me tonight that I should come here and see that you had everything you needed. I told her that I would. You don't want me to get into trouble with my mom, do you?"

She pulled back and looked at him. He let her to a point, but he didn't let her go completely. "You're afraid of your mother. Big bad Jesse Hunter is afraid of his mommy."

He grinned and pulled her back into his arms. "Of course, I am. And she's well aware of it." He held her for several minutes. She laughed at him for a minute then sighed heavily. He wanted to ask her what was wrong and he wanted to tell her that he was sorry. He didn't because he didn't want to upset her again. When she relaxed, he held her tighter and, when he realized she was asleep, he could have danced a jig. Instead, he pulled the blankets tighter around them and closed his eyes. As he drifted off to sleep, he knew that this was the place he wanted to spend the rest of his life. Right here, holding this woman in his arms.

Chapter 16

She didn't know what had awakened her, and she tried to snuggle deeper into the blankets to hide from it. When something hit her hard, she cried out.

"You slut." Joey saw the woman there, but couldn't believe her eyes. "You simply will spread your legs for whatever comes around you, won't you? Get out of that bed and get your bottom home right now."

"Grandmother?" Joey looked around for Jesse and saw his jacket and coat lying on the chair. "What did you do with Jesse?"

"So that's his name, is it? Probably some lowlife that will knock you up and leave you at the first chance he gets. I thought I told you to do something." She raised the cane again, and Joey flinched away. When it didn't hit her, she peeked around her arm to see Jesse standing there, holding it from hitting her.

"You touch her with this again, and I will show you what it feels like. Now you'll step away from her or, so help me, I'll forget all the teaching my mother beat into my head about never hitting a woman."

Grandmother snorted but moved back. "You'll regret

155

that, young man. She's not worth it. Ask anyone in town."

Joey's grandmother had raised her when her parents had died. She'd never approved of her mother, saying that she'd driven her son to his death and any number of other things she'd felt she'd done. Joey's mother wasn't a great mom, forgetting she had a daughter for the most part, but she'd loved Joey's dad.

"Jesse Hunter, this is my grandmother, Josephine Foster. Grandmother, this is Jesse Hunter. He was just leaving." He moved to the chair, pushed it to the side of her bed, and sat down. She glared at him but didn't think he cared.

"I want to know what you think you're doing running up a bill as if you have money. You have nothing left of your inheritance. Your mother saw to that." Grandmother sat in the other chair as if she was queen, and all should bow before her. "I will take you home with me, and we'll forget this whole running away thing ever happened."

"I didn't run away. I left. Well, that's not true; you kicked me out the day I turned eighteen. No money, no transportation, and not even my clothes. You *gave* me what I had on to teach me a lesson." Joey hated airing this in front of Jesse after he'd been so kind to stay with her last night. "And if you think I'm going back to that hell hole, you're nuttier than I thought you were."

The cane came down hard, and she nearly cowered from the noise. "You'll treat me with respect or, so help me, I'll teach you how to do so."

"You must earn respect before you should expect to get it. A good friend of mine told me that once."

Grandmother snorted again, this time at Jesse. "Some liberal arts major that hasn't worked a day in his life, I bet.

You, young man, will stay out of this. This is family business, and you are most assuredly not family." She looked at Joey again. "I believe I have instructed you several times to get dressed. I'm not going to say so again. I have a few places I would like to stop at before we head—"

"The liquor stores are closed on Sundays. You'll either have to buy your stuff at a convenience store or wait until tomorrow." Joey looked over at Jesse, shocked. She didn't know that he was aware of her grandmother, much less that she had a drinking problem. "And as for not being family, that's incorrect as well. I'm going to marry Joey, if she'll have me."

Joey, he'd called her Joey for the first time since she'd meet him. Joey looked at her grandmother, who looked as if she had swallowed a lemon as she glared at him.

"You'll do no such thing. I won't have it." The cane hit the floor again. "You, sir, are an impertinent boy who needs to be taught how to respect his elders. Your mother should be beaten for letting you get by with so much."

Before Jesse could speak, someone came through the door. Jesse grinned when his mom stood there. She hadn't noticed Grandmother or chose to ignore her, because Annamarie went to her son and was kissed on her cheek, then she sat on Joey's bed. "You look better, dear. Did you sleep well? It's not easy sleeping in a hospital, is it?" When she winked at her, Joey knew that she was ignoring her grandmother. "Oh, Jesse, your brother is bringing you a clean suit in. He said you had two meetings today, and I'm going to sit with—" The cane hitting the floor three times in a row cut Annamarie off. "Well, hello there. Who are you?"

Grandmother stood up and pointed her cane at her. "I

am this slut's grandmother, and I am here to take her home to where she can cause no more of this tomfoolery. And this boy claims that he is to wed her. Well, I will not allow it. This boy needs to know where she comes from."

Annamarie nodded. "Yes. I can see that. He does have a tendency to speak his mind. There are times as his mom that I wonder if he'll ever learn to curb his tongue." She stood up as well. "He claims he's in love with her, so by rights, she's already my daughter. And being such, I want to tell you something important."

Grandmother looked like a fish out of water. Joey doubted that anyone had ever stood up to her before. When Annamarie was within a foot of her, Grandmother spoke. "You think you have something to say then spit it out, girl. I've not all day to listen to you blather around." Joey noticed the slight tremor in her voice and looked at Jesse when he sat on her bed.

"You insult my daughter again, and I will shove that cane so far up your tight ass that it will be weeks, maybe even months before you'll shit again. And when you do, you'll think of me every time a splinter passes beyond that sacred portal." Annamarie poked her in the chest. "And you come here again, I will personally see that you suffer beyond what you did to that girl over there, and I make that a solemn promise you good-for-nothing, stupid bitch. Now, if you would be so kind, Daniel, I'd like for you to escort this cow out of my sight."

Joey was surprised to see Daniel there, along with two other men. When Jesse turned to her and took her hand to his mouth, she could only stare at him. No one had ever stood up for her before, and she wasn't sure what to make of it.

"Now, that is why we're all afraid of our mother." Joey

laughed with the rest of them, but she kept a careful eye on Annamarie. He was right, his mother was just plain scary.

~~~

Joey had been so quiet when he'd left that he hadn't wanted to go. But his mom assured him that she'd take care of her. And then halfway to here, she'd called him to let him know that Joey was being released. He was ready to ask the driver to take him back when his mom spoke again.

"I'll take her to your house and get her set up. Samuel is there, isn't he?" He told her his butler wouldn't leave even after he'd fired him a dozen times a week. "That's because he loves you. Between Samuel and me, I'm sure we can get one girl settled in a bed. You want her in the guest room, don't you?"

"No, Mom, I do not. Put her in my room. If you're going to insist on doing this, then you'll do it my way. If you put her anywhere else, I'm going to be really pissed then have to move her on my own. Which might tear open her stitches. You don't want that, do you?" She was quiet for so long he was afraid he'd gone too far. He was ready to tell her to put her in any room she wanted, then he'd simply move to that room until Joey felt better, but she spoke first.

"Do you love her, Jesse? And don't give me a smart-assed answer. I want you both to be happy, and this isn't just a way for you to get someone to move in with you to have sex."

"I love her very much. And it is a great way to have sex. With the woman I love." He closed his eyes and put his head back on the seat. "I don't think she believes me when I tell her, and after meeting her grandmother, I can see why. She's a piece of work, isn't she?" She didn't bother answering, and he was still trying to wrap his head around his mother shoving a

159

cane up someone's bottom and then telling them that they'd poop out splinters. He shook his head, trying to concentrate on what mom was saying.

"…when you get home. Samuel will be thrilled to have someone else in the house to fuss over. You know how he can be."

Yes, he did. That's why Jesse was a little afraid. "Tell Samuel to behave around her. I don't want him to hurt her feelings, and they not get along. I will fire him if he can't get along with her. She's more important to me than a stuffy butler who never laughs."

That had been over two hours ago, and he still had at least another hour to go. As far as monthly meetings went, this one was proving to be the worst yet and the longest one in history. He looked at his watch again and then his cell to see if anyone had called, texted, or even sent him an invitation to play Wordfeud with them.

When everyone stood up, he realized he'd missed most of what was said. He didn't care, he wanted to go home, home to Joey. As he gathered the stuff from his office up to leave, Royce came in and sat down.

"Do you have a few minutes?"

If Jesse hadn't seen his smile, the one that always reminded him of a shit-eating grin, he might have said just a few. But he had seen it, and he wasn't amused. "Funny. I'm leaving. Tell Mom that I'm on my way." He went to the door as Royce started laughing. "And your wife is baking again, or hadn't you noticed?"

He heard him yell, "Fuck," as the elevator closed. Kasey hated to cook; in fact, she was terrible at it, but when she'd been pregnant with little Lee, she'd taken up baking. It had only lasted until he was born. This past week she'd brought some kind of baked goods in nearly every day.

He was pulling in the drive when he realized he should have stopped for roses. Or candy. Something romantic. He'd had Jay, Kasey's uncle, open the personal safe and bring him his great grandmother's ring. He'd been given it along with her home and property in England when he'd turned eighteen. Jesse opened the little box now. He'd not seen the ring since it had been willed to him and put into the safe.

His great-granddad had been a miner. And about anything else that had suited his fancy. His wife, Mable, had been just as adventurous and had brought their children with them on every job. When Mable had birthed their ninth child, she'd put her foot down, and her husband of fifteen years had settled in England. And for all the things he realized she'd given up for him to have his bit of fun, he'd bought her the ring Jesse was going to propose to Joey with.

There was a row of diamonds around the wideband, twenty-two of them as a matter of fact. They sparkled like stars in a bright night even now after all these decades. But in the center of the ring were three pearls. "Pure white as my love for you, pink as the sunset we shared, black as the midnights we created life." That inscription was in the band, and it never made sense to Jesse until now. His great-granddad had loved his wife. And if that didn't say so, Jesse James, or JJ to his friends and family, dying only hours after his love had died. Because he said if he could not stand to take a breath that did not smell of his Mable, he had nothing to live for.

Laughter. The house sounded of laughter. He went into the kitchen to find Joey sitting on a chair with her leg propped up on another, his mother sitting across from her and his butler Samuel making faces at them both. He thought he'd gone to the wrong house but for the people there.

"You're home. Good. I have a meeting in town to go to. I forgot, and Samuel here has a wonderful dinner for you both." She kissed the stodgy older man on the cheek, and, for the second time in as many minutes, Jesse was shocked. His butler blushed. "You take care of my girl here. She's very special to us all."

"We'll get along just fine now, Miss A. She and I have come to an understanding." Samuel winked at Joey then nodded to him. "We are going to get along fine."

Jesse didn't want to think he'd just been threatened by the man. He was sure he was just tired, but he would swear Samuel was telling him, *While you and I don't see things the same, the new missus and I do.*

"They let me go." He looked over at her when she spoke. "Your mother said it would be okay if I came here. I don't really have a place where it's going to be okay with my leg like—"

"Samuel?" The man answered his query. "Is dinner something that can be held, or do we need to eat it right now?" Jesse never took his eyes off Joey as he spoke. He couldn't believe how much he wanted her. Right now. If he had to send Samuel to the other end of the property to take her here, he'd do it. He needed to...it felt as if he needed to claim her.

"It can wait. I only made some stew to eat and some of those biscuits that you like. You need some time to settle Miss Joey in, I guess."

Jesse nodded. Yes, he did. He bent down and took her mouth quickly, then picked her up. He needed to get her upstairs and into his bed before he embarrassed them both.

He was nearly up the stairs when he thought of the ring in his pocket. Jesse smiled when he thought of a way to get her to say yes, and he slipped the tiny ring over his little finger.

"You're going to hurt your back. Put me down before I fall on you." He looked at her mouth without understanding what she was saying. "Jesse, are you listening to me?"

"No. I'm too busy trying to figure out how to have you naked before I get us up the stairs so that I can slide into your heat before you're settled in the bed." She snapped her mouth closed. "Then there is the added dilemma of trying to figure out if I want to eat your pussy before I come deep inside of you, or to fuck you until you come then drink from you. Which do you prefer?"

His cock ached, and, when she moaned, he had to stop walking. He suddenly had no blood above his waist. Pulling her closer, he took her mouth and knew that he'd hurt her. The small taste of blood only seemed to fuel his need for her.

He was five feet from the door, and he knew they weren't going to make it. Pressing her against the wall without breaking from her mouth, he pulled at her shirt. She was tugging as his own buttons as he buried his hands in the back of her pants and cupped her hot ass in his hands.

"Hurry," she begged him when he lifted his mouth from hers to take off her shirt and bra. Her nipples were already hard as stone and seemingly begging to be suckled.

He felt the cool air brush over his cock. She'd gotten his pants undone despite the way they were straining toward each other. Lifting her higher on his waist, she wrapped her uninjured leg around his hips as he held her other one. Moving with as much grace as he could manage with his pants at his thighs, he got them to the bedroom door and in it.

"I can't…I'm sorry, honey, but I want to be deep inside of you ten minutes ago." She was nodding as she shimmied out of the cotton pants she had on. He decided when he ripped them from her body that these were all she was ever going to wear again.

"Now. Hurry now. Please."

He didn't have to be asked again. He didn't just slide into her but became a part of her. His cock felt thicker than he'd ever felt in a woman, and he knew that when they came, it would be explosive. As he began to move, hard, quick strokes that took her breath away, he felt his climax spreading over him, taking him and simply overpowering him. When she screamed, loud, long, and that she loved him, he threw back his head and filled her with his seed, marked her with it, and claimed her. Roaring again when a second release took her, and him right along too, he knew that he would love this one woman for all of his life.

Dropping down onto her, rolling at the last minute, he took the ring off his finger and put it on her ring finger. She was asleep or unconscious, and he smiled at the thought of doing that to her. He'd ask her later. Right now, he was as content as he'd ever been.

Chapter 17

She watched as Samuel flipped the hash browns expertly. She smiled at him when he turned to look at her. She shook her head when he told her to give it a try.

"No. You'll have a bigger mess than the toast I tried to burn the house down with. I'll just be your taste-tester. I can do that without hurting anyone."

He pulled down a plate and dumped the beautifully browned potatoes onto it. She heard the toaster pop and hobbled over to get the toast and jam he'd put out for her. By the time she returned, she had two over easy eggs on her plate as well.

"You will eat all of that now, missus. You need to get better." He put a glass of juice in front of her as Jesse walked through the door.

Something she'd been avoiding for a long time hit her. She was in love with him. And probably had been since he'd come into her hospital room the first time. Then the night before, when he'd made love to her so gently. She turned away before he could see it on her face.

"Ah, so you've got Samuel eating out of your hand already, huh?" Jesse kissed her on the mouth as he walked toward the man.

"If you think to kiss me, too, young man, I'll bash your head in with my favorite skillet." Samuel held the pan up threateningly. "And she is worth having around. She doesn't scowl at me."

The cook was standing nearby, simply watching the other two men as though he were at a tennis match. She'd been surprised when Samuel had met her at the bottom of the stairs earlier and even more so when he told Cook that he would be cooking for her. She smiled when Cook took the pan and said something in what she thought was French.

Joey watched Jesse pour himself some coffee and lean against the counter. She cleared her throat. "I found this. I wanted to give it back to you." She held out the beautiful ring that had been on her finger when she'd woken this morning. "I think someone might have made a mistake."

He took another sip before answering her. "No. There was no mistake. I want you to have it."

"I don't want your things for sleeping with you." She flushed, feeling her face and neck heat up when both Cook and Samuel turned to look at her. "Here. Take it before someone gets the wrong idea."

"What idea would that be? That I love you? I hope so, and it wouldn't be a wrong idea. The best I've had in a long while, I think. You're going to marry me."

Samuel and Cook left the kitchen. She felt bad for running them out when it was so obviously their domain. She waited until the door closed behind them before she spoke again. "I'm not going to marry you. You're a very nice man, and I like—"

"I don't want to be a nice man. I want to be your husband."

He knelt down in front of her and took the ring. She was happy, but that was short-lived. "Tell me you're going to marry me, Joey."

Well, that wasn't very nice, she thought. "Why are you calling me that now?" she asked him suddenly. "Before it was 'Josephine,' and nothing else. What changed your mind?"

"Meeting your grandmother. Her name is Josephine, right?" She nodded. "And...did she ever hit you with that cane? Before yesterday, did she ever hit you with it?"

She looked away, not able to tell him while he was staring at her so intently. "Yes. She thought it would cure me. I didn't...most of the time she was so drunk she'd miss for the most part, but she'd catch me too. I suppose it could have been worse. It ended up only being a three year, seven month, fourteen-day sentence." She looked at him, horrified at what she'd said out loud.

"Cure you of what?"

His voice was so soft that she couldn't help but answer him. If he had demanded, she would have simply changed the subject like she always did. "School was difficult for me. Not because I couldn't make the grades; that was easy, but keeping myself...lower. At first, I'd wanted to make her like me. You know, have her not regret that she'd taken me in when no one else would?" She turned in the seat and propped her leg on the other chair, not really needing it, but it was easier to talk without seeing Jesse. "The first time I'd brought home an A, I'd been so proud. It hadn't been hard, you see. I can see the words forever once I read them or hear them. But she'd accused me of cheating. That was the first time she'd... hit me." She'd not only hit her but had beaten her. Badly. It had taken her over a week to be able to go back to school, and

167

a lot longer before she realized that it wasn't her fault that she'd been hurt.

"How old were you? And why did she think you cheated?" She snorted at his questions. "Joey?"

"It was about a month after my parents had died. I was fourteen. And why did she think I cheated?" Joey closed her eyes, remembering her grandmother standing over her with the cane held up high. "She said that I was a good-for-nothing female and an ugly one at that. And if I was to get caught putting on airs, she'd let them take me to prison and let me rot there. It was my mother's fault that I was like I was." Joey had found out a few months later that her mother had been like her. Or at least she was like her mother. A photographic memory, the school had told her. When she'd been tested to go into high school, she'd been the only one to finish the standardized tests. And had asked if she could read a book while the rest had finished. She'd been sent home instead. That was the second beating. The one that she'd had to hide from nearly everyone, it had been so bad. It had taken months for some of the bruises to heal, and longer still for the fear to subside.

"Then, when? Was it every time you tried to better yourself?" She nodded. "I should have killed the fucking bitch when I had that fucking cane in my hand."

She stared at him open-mouthed, then snapped it closed before she answered. "She would have hit you back. When you weren't looking or asleep, she'd sneak into your room and hit you. There were times when I'd sleep with a chair under the knob so she couldn't come in. But soon she started putting me in a room with just walls and a door. There were no locks, no windows to escape. I had to..." She stood up quickly. "I have to go."

He stood as well. "Where? I can take you wherever you want. Or Samuel can. I think he'd enjoy it."

As if on cue, Samuel and Cook walked in, and they were arguing. Again. They'd been doing that since she came in. Both men smiled at her then frowned at Jesse.

"You'll be late if you don't hurry your bottom along, and your mother will blame me. You'd best have Michael run you in. I've already called him." Samuel took off his clean apron as he started fussing with Jesse's coat before helping him put it on. "Be off. We'll keep your miss entertained today. We might even take her with us to play our chess in the park."

Jesse kissed her again. This time, he pulled her fully into his arms and held her before setting her away. His cock had been hard, and she could see him tugging his coat around him as he went out the door. Joey looked over at Cook.

"The ring looks lovely on your hand, miss. You will make Mr. Jesse very happy. He needs a woman in his life."

She looked down at her hand and was surprised to see that he'd slipped it back on her finger. She was going to kill the man. As soon as he walked in the door, she was going to kill him. Sitting down hard, she remembered that she wanted to go to Patty's graveside and asked Cook if it was possible that she could call a cab.

"No cab comes here, miss. We have the big gates, and also there are many cars for you to have a ride in. I take. Or Samuel. We will serve you in any way you need."

~~~

Doyle watched the young man come into the building. He'd been waiting for an hour, not really sure when the owners would show up. He'd half expected them to show up at noon or later. Here it was just after seven in the morning and, as far as he could tell, he was the last Hunter to arrive. The security guard nodded to him, and Jesse came toward him.

"They said you're here to see me. I'm sorry, Doyle, but I have a meeting in about five minutes that I can't miss. It's with...it's about Joey and what's going on."

The man looked worried, and Doyle was glad to see it. He'd take care of his girl. "I have some news on that front too. If you would let me walk with you, I'll explain it to you." Doyle liked this man but was sure that all he saw was a large, bald man who owned a bar. Doyle liked to think he was more than that but also liked the low profile he kept. It had helped him gather the information he had to give this man.

"All right. We'll take the elevator up." He started past the desk and paused to speak to the man there. "Jay, could you please call my mom and tell her I'm here? And will you also give Mr. O'Donnell a visitor badge so he can come up with me?"

Doyle was asked to show his ID. He hesitated for a few seconds and finally pulled it out. And then showed them that he was armed as they'd seen his carry permit. He heard Jesse say something that sounded like, "mother fuck" under his breath but didn't comment. He was planning to tell him anyway. They were in the elevator when the younger man spoke.

"You're the Feds. Why are you pretending to be a bartender? Or is this all a scam to get something from...hell, I have no idea. What the fuck is going on?"

"I'm not pretending. I own the bar. Have since I retired about ten years ago. I only started paying attention to the things going on around Joey since she came in one night beaten to shit and back. She said she'd been mugged. Took me about a week to figure out what had really happened." The doors opened then, and Doyle saw two men that he knew from the Bureau and one he did not. They shook hands and Doyle was suddenly a part of the team.

"Who hit her?" Jesse asked as soon as it was understood that Doyle wasn't a visitor so much as an informant. "You said she'd been beaten and you found out from whom. So, who hit her?"

Doyle took measure of the younger man. He wanted to hate him or, at the very least, dislike him some, but couldn't. He thought the guy genuinely liked Joey if he didn't already love her. He nodded, knowing that what he said here today was going to either change his mind or not.

"She has a grandmother. Probably already met her." Jesse nodded that he had, as did the other three men. "She's a lot worse than you've probably heard or seen. When Joey lived there, she was little more than a servant. The old bitch wouldn't let her spread her wings and fly so when Joey turned eighteen, she lit out like the house was burning around her."

"We talked to a few of her neighbors. They said that Joey had been an issue with the grandmother and felt that if she hadn't taken a heavy hand, the girl would have ended up on the wrong end of a slab in a funeral home." Doyle shook his head as Levy spoke. "You saying ten neighbors lied?"

"No. They probably told you what they'd been told. Joey wasn't in the house most of the time…not so's anyone could see her. She had to live in a single room in the basement and then when she wasn't there, she was cleaning, toting, or catering to the woman. I got my information from the hospital where she'd end up when the girl wouldn't do something that the grandmother demanded. Guess there were times when Joey'd be brought in, and the grandmother would take her home without medical care. Only reason she'd end up in the emergency room in the first place is 'cause she'd collapse somewhere from the pain."

Doyle reached into his pocket and tossed an envelope on the table between them. He didn't speak as they went through the pictures and the testimonies from the staff he'd been able to interview. Jesse looked at several of the pictures and got up to pace. Doyle changed his opinion of the kid. He *was* a keeper.

"You don't think this thing with Patty and Joey has anything to do with her grandmother, do you?"

Doyle shook his head at Jesse as he paced.

"Then why bring her up? I mean, I want this information, but why here, why now?"

"The grandmother is in town, right?" He knew she was so didn't wait for an answer. "If she gets to Joey before the Jennings woman does, she will hurt her enough that Joey will be less likely to defend herself. Or she'll sell her granddaughter to the bitch to have something more to spend on booze."

Jesse stopped pacing and looked at him. The two of them seemed to connect then. Doyle knew that Jesse would do whatever it took to keep Joey safe. Whatever and however he needed to do it.

"So, do you know where Jennings is?" Levy asked. "We know that she killed a woman last night, but—"

"Killed a woman? When was this?" Jesse cursed a blue streak that had one of the men flush.

Yeah, Doyle thought he liked this kid.

172

"You'd better start giving me information I can work with or, so help me, I'll call your boss and have Doyle put on the case. He seems to have a handle on this better than you three do, and he's fucking retired."

"You give me a job with your firm when this is done, and I'll take the case." Doyle looked at Jesse only. This was what he'd come here for. "I've got it okay, but I want more. A job with loss prevention with your company, and I'm all yours."

"Done." Jesse took his hand and shook it. And just like that, Doyle worked for the Hunter Corporation. "Now, let's get these bitches so I can take my girl and get married."

Doyle knew about the dead woman. Sally Ferguson had been killed coming from the ATM minutes after the Jennings woman had had her card taken. The Feds were waiting on her to use the credit cards they thought were still in the purse when it had been taken. The pictures on the cell phone, the one that had been covered in blood, had told the story better than words. Doyle looked around the room

"She's staying at the hotel on route forty. There's a guy with her and, best I can figure, it's her brother-in-law." He watched one of the other agents get up and walk toward a map that had been laid out on another table. Doyle followed and pointed to the place. "She's been there since the fire. He's been coming and going for a bit now. I think he or the woman killed a man by the name of Stanton. His body turned up in the morgue a few days ago."

"How do you know they're related? The murdered man and Sondra?" Doyle looked at Jesse and shrugged. "A hunch? Okay, I can live with that. You've had more information than these three have. So, who was he?"

"Guy that sold himself off as a hitman. Wasn't much

more than a hooker. He'd talk a big game; hell, I heard it myself when he'd sit in the bar. Anyway, he came in about three days before his body came up and told me how he'd scammed this man and his sister. He said he didn't care to fuck her, but the guy he'd let do whatever he wanted in any part of him he liked. When he was found…let's just leave it at he'd gotten his wish apparently."

He'd had sex. Before or after his death, the examiners weren't sure. Jon Stanton had been sodomized horribly and not just with a dick, but whatever the other person had been able to reach as well. Doyle had talked to the coroner and was told that the man had not gone peacefully.

"So this brother-in-law? Is he still hanging around, or we gonna find him lying in some ditch too?" Goldman, the other agent, had an attitude that needed adjusting, and Doyle was about ready to do it for him free of charge. But Jesse beat him to it.

"You find anything more than this man has, and you can speak; otherwise, you go sit at the table and shut the fuck up. Had you been on the case half what this man has been, a woman wouldn't be dead, and my fiancée wouldn't be shot."

Doyle nearly laughed out loud when the other man sputtered but caught himself. He thought he was going to enjoy working for this man.

"Let me ask you something," Jesse said while the other men organized a hit on the hotel an hour later. "Why didn't you come with this information sooner? You had it all right there. Why not go to the police?"

"Did. Someone from their department…" He pointed to the man sitting at the table that Jesse has sent there. "He shit in their oatmeal at the beginning. Told them when they wanted podunks to help out, he'd give them a call. Didn't set well with the department. When I went to them, I wasn't aware of this yet. I told them all I had, and it wasn't until I was called to the Ferguson scene that one of the cops told me. Thought maybe I could get to the right person on my own."

Doyle watched Jesse seem to process this. When he nodded, Doyle knew that whatever the man did, he'd hate to be in Goldman's position when he was finished. The younger man was quiet, but Doyle was reasonably sure that he could get results better that way than screaming. And he knew that when Jesse was finished, heads were going to roll. Doyle hoped he'd be around to see it when they did.

Chapter 18

Sondra watched the bar. The stupid girl worked here, didn't she? When the hell was she going to show up? Or did she think money just grew on trees? Probably. Homeless bitch was making her life difficult at the moment, and she wanted her gone.

Sondra looked down at her list. She'd worked on it most of the night and was quite proud of it. She knew that two things hinged on making it work, and killing the girl was on the top. Then number two was to make nice with the elder Hunter woman.

That was going to be a piece of cake, she figured. Annamarie wouldn't want to lose her as a friend because of her connections with the real estate market, and Sondra thought that alone was going to be her ticket. People like the Hunters needed more land to suck the economy up. Then there was the fact that she'd saved her life. Sondra knew that Annamarie had been out of it most of the time they'd been in the building, and once the homeless bitch was dead and unable to refute her claims, Sondra would simply convince her that she'd been the one to save her and there had been no one else there.

The third thing on her list made her frown. She wasn't sure how she was going to be able to explain the dead woman. Sondra had read the papers this morning and saw that the stupid bitch had taken her picture. The police said that they were searching for a woman in the pictures to ask her some questions. Could she please come to the station so they could "get a clearer picture of what had happened"? Like that was bloody going to happen.

A car, a large SUV actually, pulled in front of the bar. She'd seen that car before and was laughingly aware that it didn't belong to the homeless bitch. She watched as a man got out and went to the door, then back to the car. It drove off a few minutes later. Sondra came out of her hiding place and went to see what it was.

Nothing that she could see. She remembered the man bending and wondered if he'd slipped something under the door. Bending down, she looked and saw that he had. There was something a good five or so inches from the door. Sondra cursed at the man's efficiency. He couldn't have just slid it under; no, the moron had to shove it under there like he was trying for the gold. She stomped back to her hiding place.

The list was not going to work if she couldn't get the stupid girl. Sondra waited for a little while longer until she remembered the paper she'd taken. No one was using it, sitting on the front porch of that house, so she didn't even feel bad. Opening it, she was disappointed that there was nothing on the front page about her. She'd take care of that soon enough. She was going to be the top salesperson in the state when this was done. Annamarie was going to be standing there right next to her too.

Seeing an obit about Patty Melbourne and turning to the

page, Sondra laughed at what it said. No wonder no one was coming here, they were at the woman's funeral. She tossed the paper on the ground and made her way to the city limits. This stupid bar was out a ways, and she was exhausted when she got to a place where she could get a ride.

She still had ten bucks left of the measly twenty the other woman had given her, and she wondered if she should go to the bank again. Sondra decided that she could go to a convenience store and buy something and tell the cashier she wanted more cash. The woman...Sally Ferguson according to the credit card she now had, owed her more than Sondra had gotten from her anyway.

The place was a rundown on the inside as it had looked on the outside. There was a long counter that had two registers on it and also a couple of free-standing ones that held coffee and pop, respectively. Sondra went to the coffee one and made herself a cup of creamy latte with hazelnut flavoring. She was taking a sip when she walked to the counter. It wasn't great, but it was the best she'd had since this thing with Annamarie had started.

"That'll be four-ten."

Sondra raised a brow at the price but didn't comment. She handed him the credit card and asked about getting more cash. He told her to tell the machine that.

How much? She wanted to clean out her account, but the biggest choices she had was fifty bucks. Thinking if she needed more, she'd simply come back; she pressed that key. The machine immediately asked for a pin. She didn't have one. Before she could come up with a plausible reason she didn't, the sales clerk told her to put it as credit and not debit, and she'd be okay.

He handed her the cash and told her to have a great day. It wasn't until she was outside that she remembered the coffee. She almost turned around to go in and get it when a cop pulled up in front of the place and got out. Hurrying now, she went to the first restaurant she could find and went inside to use the phone.

The ride to the cemetery wasn't all that long, but it did cost her twelve dollars. The driver glared at her when she didn't give him a tip. Like she gave a shit. She was on a mission, and it didn't mean she was going to spend her little bit of money making some jerk who sat on his ass all day richer. She was going to the grave of the woman she'd killed. She pulled out the little gun she'd found at the hotel that day.

Killing Patty hadn't been what she'd planned. Her plan had been to hurt the homeless bitch enough to drag her off somewhere and make her suffer. But the older woman had stepped in front of the bitch just as Sondra had fired. At first, when she'd hit her, she simply thought that she'd dropped for cover and fired three more times to get her to rise up. But she'd missed twice and then hit the bitch in the leg, causing her to drop out of sight too before she heard the shouts. Some big guy had come around the corner of the building just as Sondra had a bead on bitch's head. She might have shot him too, but the little gun was empty. She had since loaded it and now carried more of the cute little bullets in her pocket everywhere she went. Smiling, she thought one never knew when someone was going to piss you off, so it was good to be prepared.

There were three people there at the gravesite, but Sondra didn't see the bitch. There were two men, one she recognized as a minister from the paper and another younger man she didn't know. There was the same SUV there, black and huge sitting nearby, but she couldn't tell if anyone was in it yet or not. Moving to just within fifty feet of the men, she stepped behind a large tree just as the door to the SUV opened. It was the man from the bar.

Sondra watched as he fussed with his coat. Then he walked around the other side of the thing and opened that door. When he and a woman started to walk away, Sondra had a moment of surprise when she realized that she was looking at the homeless bitch. What the hell was she doing in a car like this with a butler, no less?

Anger had always made her stupid, she knew this. But today she was pegged in the red with anger, and she didn't stop to think about what she was doing. She moved up beside the man and woman and fired twice. The man dropped, and the woman turned on her. Sondra pointed the gun at her, and everyone there stopped.

"You've fucked up my life enough. With you dead, I can get everything back in order and get to selling houses again." The girl looked at her as if she didn't have a clue. "When I kill you. When I kill you, everything will be back to normal again."

"I don't know who you are. Why don't you let me see to Lowell first, and you can tell me what this is all about." Rage surged through Sondra, and she turned the gun on the man lying there. "Don't."

The girl was actually going to order her around? That was not going to happen. Sondra heard something behind her and, before she could fire at the man again, she was rushed from the side. As she went over her head then landed hard on her back, she heard the police sirens going off. Putting the gun to the man who laid over her head, she told him to get off her. He moved, but not before he elbowed her several times. She thought about shooting him on principle but didn't know how many cops were coming or if they were coming to get her.

When she stood up, the bitch was holding her hands over the man she'd come with. It looked like she'd gotten him in the arm, but couldn't be sure. And the police were getting closer.

"Get in that thing over there. We're going to leave here right fucking now. What I have plans for, you won't—"

"I'm not going anywhere with you. I remember you now. You were the bitch from the fire. You tried to kill me."

Sondra smiled. Finally, she was getting it.

"You can go fuck yourself for all I give a shit."

The gun exploded in her hand. She hadn't even realized she'd fired the thing, and she was pretty sure it had gone off more than once. She was just glad that the idiot that had rushed her hadn't been able to disarm her or knock the gun away. The girl fell back, and Sondra hoped that she'd killed her, but when she got up and came after her, Sondra had to take several steps back before she could fire again. There should have been one more bullet, but it only snapped at her.

Sondra fell back as the bitch punched her. She felt the blood pour from her nose, and when she tried to get up to fight back, the girl kicked her in the head. Dizzy for several seconds and not able to see, she fell back again when another kick hit her in the ribs. The bitch wasn't waiting for her to get up.

"You should have shot me when you had the chance. Now I'm going to make you hurt like you did me." The girl was speaking gibberish, and Sondra knew it. She'd never hurt the girl without needing to. She made it sound as if Sondra had tried to strangle her because she enjoyed killing. She most certainly did not.

"You should have died in that fire. All this…" She waved her hand around the cemetery. "This is all your fault. All you had to do was let me kill Annamarie so that I could collect the insurance money. Or you could have let me kill you, and the effect would have been the same. Double the money."

She smiled. It all made perfect sense, and if she didn't see that, then the girl was stupider than she'd first thought. Car doors opened behind them, and Sondra just knew that the police had arrived. When no one came to see to her wounds, she looked at the girl again. She was shaking her head.

"You're nuts. I'm sure you know that, but you're really nuts. The police are looking for you. Hell, even the Feds. If you think this is going to go away because you want it to, then—"

"The Feds? What on earth do they want to do with me?" Sondra pulled some bullets out of her pocket and started to load her gun. "I haven't done a thing wrong for them to want to speak to me. Unless it's to tell them what a fuck up you are. But I'm going to save them the trouble of that in a moment."

The girl laughed. Long and hard. Sondra wasn't sure what she found so funny but smiled too. This was going to be easy. Much easier than she'd thought. When the gun was reloaded, Sondra had to wipe the blood off it before she could get a better grip on it. She was just raising it to fire when she felt something touch her head. Then someone jerked her gun out of her slippery hands.

"Move, and I will happily end your fucking life."

She knew that voice and started to turn to the younger man.

"I mean it. I will have no problem whatsoever putting this entire clip into your head."

"Jesse, if you don't put that gun away and let me finish this, you're going to be in such trouble with your mother. What will she think when I tell her you were dropping the F-bomb as if you had a potty mouth?" She tried again to turn and found she couldn't. "Stop this right now. I won't sell your company any more property if you don't stop this nonsense right this moment."

"She thinks that once I'm dead, your mom will come back to her as if nothing happened. I think she's lost her marbles somewhere along the line."

Sondra glared at the bitch.

"She keeps talking like I should feel privileged that she has picked me to die."

"You're not dying. She might, but you're not."

Sondra started to protest when she saw a pair of dark pants in front of her.

"Sondra Jennings, you're under arrest for the murder of Clint Hampton, Sally Ferguson, and Patty Melbourne, also the attempted murder of Annamarie Hunter and Josephine Foster."

"Who? I don't know any Ferguson or Foster. You got the wrong person for those and if you find that other guy, Jon somebody, I didn't kill him either. Clint did that because he fucked him."

The bitch knelt down in front of her and was grinning. "I'm Joey Foster, you mental case. I hope you get the chair for this."

The police jerked her to her feet, and before she could tell them that they had the wrong person, again, she was told if she spoke again, it had better be to say she wanted a lawyer. She looked over at Jesse and raised a brow. "Will you represent me? I've been using the Hunters for my entire career. Tell these men yes so that I can get this thing over with."

Jesse walked toward her and smiled. "Fuck off, you miserable excuse for a human being. You tried to kill my mother and my fiancée. Why on earth would I help you get off?"

Before she could answer him, she was being dragged to a cruiser. Fiancée? What the fuck? He couldn't be thinking of marrying that homeless person, could he? She was in the back of the cruiser when she found her tongue. The driver, a big cop, told her to shut up or he'd shut her up. She was so going to report him.

~~~

Jesse gathered Joey into his arms and held her. When she tried to pull away, he asked…no, he begged her for just a few more minutes. He looked over at his friend and cook and smiled when he tried to brush the blood off his suit.

Joey turned in his arms enough to see Lowell. "He said he had a gun in his other suit when I tried to help him. I nearly wet myself laughing. Do you think he was serious?"

"Probably. He told me once he was a hitman for the now defunct mob. I thought at the time he'd been kidding about it until someone tried to rob us when we'd been out Christmas shopping. He saved my life."

The ambulance attendant came to stand next to them. He had the strangest look on his face, a cross between a grin and adoration. "Mr. Melbourne said that you hit that woman like

185

a man. Said he would like to see you fight sometime. You really knock her on her ass with one punch?"

Joey flushed, and Jesse laughed. "Yes, I did. She was trying to hurt that man over there. And I only fight when it's necessary. Is Mr. Melbourne all right?"

"Yeah. He said his head hurts, but that's his own fault. We're going to take him in, so it's not a waste. That fancy guy, he said he's driving you home. Might not want to let him behind the wheel. He lost a bit of blood."

Jesse told Lowell to get in the ambulance, or he'd fire him. After several more threats, he told him he was calling Samuel. That shut him up and sent him to the ambulance. He and Joey followed them to the hospital in the truck. He couldn't let her go just yet.

JESSE

Chapter 19

Joey was sitting in the outer office of the big building two days later. She had been staying with Jesse and was being pampered by his staff and having sex every night with him in that huge bed. She shifted on the soft couch and thought about this morning. Christ, that man could do things to her body that made her melt.

He'd been in the shower when she'd woken up. She thought maybe she'd make the bed. Actually, she'd wanted to snatch a pillowcase, the one he'd been sleeping on, but he'd come out of the bathroom before she could.

"We're just going to mess it up again now that you're awake." He came up behind her and wrapped his hands around her waist. "If you help me do that, I'll make it worth your while."

His voice was a purr, and she felt it all the way to her toes. When she tried to say something, she'd lost her train of thought when he cupped her pussy.

"You're wet, aren't you? I want you to open your pants for me and let me see." She started to shake her head when he lifted her breast with his other hand and pinched her nipple. "Open them, Joey. Let me run my fingers through your curls

187

and then taste what I find there."

Her fingers shook as she worked the button. The zipper slid down quickly, and, as soon as she moved her hands, he slid his hand down the front of her panties. His moan made her try to close her thighs when she felt herself get wetter. His "no, wider" had her spreading her legs for him.

"Jesse, please. We shouldn't be doing this. You have to go to work." Instead of answering her, he lifted her shirt up and cupped her bare breast. "Please."

"Please, what? Tell me how you want me to please you, baby, and I will." She felt his finger touch her clit and she moaned. "You want me to suck you here? Taste that cream that you give to me? I would love that. Turn for me and lay down."

She did as he said and saw that his towel was gone, and his cock stood straight from his groin. Leaning in, she took a quick lick of his own cream and heard him growl at her. He didn't speak but pushed her back away. She lay down and watched as he gripped his cock. She thought he was going to come on her and touched her pussy.

"Strip down and let me see you naked. I want to see all of you when you come like this." Her shirt was already gone, and she'd not put on a bra, needing a shower. "Take it off and then spread those lovely legs for me so I can watch you play."

She'd never touched herself before, only in the shower to get clean, but was looking forward to doing it for him. Without getting off the bed, she shimmied out of her jeans, taking her panties with them. Not sure what to do next, she put her feet on the edge of the bed and let her legs fall open. His hiss of breath made her pussy wetter.

Touching her clit was harder than she'd thought it would

be. So she watched his face as she experimented. When his eyes seemed to glaze over, she knew she had a part of it right. The first time her fingernail slipped over her clit, she moaned and lifted her ass up higher with her feet. Jesse's breath on her thigh startled her.

"Don't stop. Please don't stop what you're doing." She looked down her body at him. He was looking at her pussy so intently that she nearly came. "I'm going to fuck you while you play, fuck you with my tongue until you come in my mouth."

"I'm so close now it won't take much. The thought of your tongue dancing in me makes me so wet." She watched as he slowly lowered his head. "Suck me, Jesse, please. Make me come in your mouth, then I want you to fuck me with your cock."

His mouth covered hers, and she screamed out. His fingers joined hers and his tongue until she felt him slide down to her tiny puckered hole. As soon as he rubbed his finger over it and popped through the tight rings, she came, screaming out his name, not even caring if anyone heard her. Before her body was finished, still jerking and tightening, he stood up.

She reached for him, sitting up and taking him into her mouth before he could speak. He fucked her mouth a few times before he pulled back and stood there.

"On your knees. I want to take you from behind and hard. Christ, I want to fuck you hard." She was barely the way he'd told her before his cock was deep in her pussy. His fingers dug deep into her hip, and she knew she'd have a mark. When he leaned over her and nipped at her shoulder, she came again, screaming louder this time than the last. As soon as she started to slam back with his every surge forward, he bit her again and then stood up. She lowered her head to the bed to try to brace herself for his hard pounding. When he came, he cried out that he loved her, then reached around her body to her clit and pinched, making her come again.

And now here she was, waiting to talk to the police again, and then she was leaving. She looked around the beautiful room and wondered what a man like Jesse saw in this sterile room. His office, she knew, wasn't much different.

There was a desk, a reception area he'd called it, with a woman sitting behind it. She was busy answering calls and directing people to where they wanted to go. She had sent one man away when she'd informed him four times that Mrs. Hunter wasn't going to be able to see him today, that he'd have to call for another appointment. The man shut up when the security officers showed up with their hands on their weapons.

There were no plants to speak of. Three by the window, and that was all. And those seemed to be sickly and not all that happy to be here. The one nearest the window looked like it was thirsty, and the larger one, the one that was seemingly growing up the window, needed to be repotted badly. She wondered if she asked the pretty lady there if she could do it if she'd have her thrown out as well. There was a small plant, and Joey thought maybe it was the healthiest of the three, which wasn't saying much. She could tell even from here that someone had put out a cigarette in the dirt. She wanted to find the person and put one out on him. Appalled by her train of thought, she looked up when she heard her name.

"They'll see you now, Miss Foster."

She stood up and put her hands in her pockets. That's when she remembered the ring.

"Could you please see that Mr. Jesse gets this back? I tried to give it to him twice now, and he keeps putting it back. I think he's nuts." She flushed when the woman stepped back from her and the ring. But her smile made her think she wasn't mad.

"It's been in his family for a long while, so I'm pretty sure if he gave it to you, he meant for you to keep it." She smiled again. "I take it he hasn't popped the question that usually goes with a ring like that, has he?"

"Popped? No. He's ordered and told me what he thinks he wants, but I think it was just the sex. He seemed to…" She shut up, knowing that she was babbling and embarrassing herself. "I'm sorry. I don't know why I told you that."

"You needed to, that's why." She looked around and told Joey to follow her. She led her to another door and knocked before going in. "Here. You need to speak to these ladies. I'll tell the gentlemen that you're busy at the moment."

Joey found herself inside the office, and the door shut before she could say anything. She turned to the room when she heard a small laugh.

This room was vastly different than any of the others she'd been in. this one was an office that she could work in if she was an office sort of person. The plants were healthy and green. The windows were huge and bright with sunshine, and the furniture looked like the woman who came toward her. Well, both women. The younger Hunter women, as a matter of fact.

"I heard you were coming in today. Annamarie is upset that she couldn't be here when you spoke to the Feds. She seemed to think you were going to kick some ass and take names later. Have a seat."

Joey didn't want to sit. She wanted to give someone this ring and leave before she did something really stupid, like tell Jesse Hunter she was in love with him.

"If you could, please take this thing." She held out the ring again. "I'll be on my merry little way, and everyone can move on with their lives."

"It won't work," the other woman, she thought her name was Kylie, said. "You can try to get away from the Hunter family, but they keep coming back for you. I tried several times before I finally admitted that I needed him in my life."

"I don't want him in my life. I was doing just fine before. And I don't want to talk any more about that stupid cunt that...sorry, Mrs. Jennings anymore."

Both women laughed.

"No, you had it right. Sondra Jennings is a cunt." This from Kasey, Royce's wife. "You didn't sit. I wish you would. I just spoke to Royce, and he said your grandmother is trying to bargain with them about you."

Joey sat. She'd assumed this was about the other woman, not her grandmother. "What has she to bargain about me with? I'm not going back there if that's what he thinks. I'm going to move into my own place soon enough, and I'm never going to let her find me again."

"Your own place? I thought you were going to move in with Jesse?" Joey was shaking her head before Kylie finished. "Then, where are you two living? I assumed, well, we all assumed you and he were getting married. Thus the ring."

Joey put the ring on the table next to her. "I can't marry him, and you guys know it. And since we've established that I'm having sex with him, I can tell you right off that there is little sleep involved. He is a lawyer, for Christ's sake.

What does he want with a college dropout who doesn't have two nickels, hell, not even two cents to rub together?" She stood up again. "Tell him that he doesn't' have to listen to my grandmother. She's nothing more than a drunk and an abusive bitch."

She was nearly to the door when Kasey spoke again. "She told him that you beat her. That you were the abusive person and that most times she feared for her life."

She turned slowly back to the women. "Does he believe her?"

"I don't believe so," Kasey said quietly. "Why don't you go and find out? Jesse Hunter is a good man, Joey, and I believe he loves you a great deal. And if he doesn't love you that much already, then he is fast getting there."

Her heart was breaking, and she wasn't sure what to do. She knew her grandmother hated her but had never known the extent of it. She leaned her head against the door she'd turned back to. "I love him. I think I...I think I was born to love him and now...I don't understand this."

"Understand what, Joey? Why he can love you? I'm sure any one of us could give you a starting list." She shook her head at Kasey's question. "Then is it your grandmother? If so, then you can do something about that right now before the old bitch dies. Ask her. When my mother died, there was so much I wanted to tell her. I know what you have to say to that old bitch isn't the same, but if you can, say it now."

Without turning around, she spoke. "When my parents died, it really didn't mean all that much to me. It was more like I'd lost a long lost uncle and aunt than my parents. They didn't want me, I'm not even sure why they had me, but they were so involved that they ignored me for the most part. When it was beneficial to them, they'd dress me up and parade me in front of their friends. Then they were killed. I had to go and live with my grandmother then. I was excited. I didn't even know I had a grandmother until the week before I moved in." Joey laughed bitterly. "That lasted until I crossed over the threshold. She hit me with her cane the second the man who'd brought me there left. It didn't get any better as the years went on."

"Someone should have come back to ask you if you were fairing alright. What did you tell them when they did?"

"What I needed to tell them to survive." She opened the door. "I'm going to do this, but not for her or him. I'm doing this for me. Then I'm leaving, and I want you all to leave me alone."

She didn't wait for them to speak but left the room. She thought she heard someone say, "You go, girl," but couldn't' be sure. This time, when she went to the door that she knew belonged to Jesse, she simply opened it on her own and slammed it behind her.

"You fucking bitch. How many times do I have to tell you to leave me the fuck alone?"

Her grandmother stood up and raised her cane up. Before she moved, though, she seemed to change her mind and sat back down hard. She turned to the men sitting there and wiped at her cheek. Joey didn't think the woman could cry unless she heard the words "last call" at her favorite bar.

"See what I was telling you? She's so abusive to me. But she's all I have in my golden years, and without her help, I just don't know...even with all her hurtful words and meanness, I need someone to watch over me in the event I fall."

Joey saw Mrs. Hunter roll her eyes, and Daniel cover his

mouth. She thought maybe they were laughing. She didn't look at Jesse, not sure what he was doing. But Royce stood up and came toward her. She flinched away when he reached for her.

"I'm going to show you to your seat," he said quietly. "I swear none of us Hunters will cause you any harm." She looked over his shoulder at Jesse.

"Are you sure about that?" Jesse looked ready to kill and, since he was looking right at her, she thought maybe he was mad at her. Royce looked at his brother then back at her with a wink.

"Right before you came in, she was telling us how you would take her pension checks and blow it on drugs. Want to come and listen to the fairy tale with us?" He handed her off to Jesse, who took her hand. "Let her sit next to you. Maybe between the two of you, one or both of you won't end up going to prison for murdering this lying bitch."

Royce moved away as Jesse continued to look at her. Before she could figure out what he wanted, he pulled her into his arms. He only held her to him, and it felt like nothing she'd ever felt before. When he tilted her chin up, and she looked at him, he smiled.

"I love you, Joey Foster. And will for the rest of our days. I want to ask you something I should have days ago. And even though now is not the time, I need to ask you now so that I can clear this up before much more time goes by. Okay?" She nodded. "Joey, will you please run our new greenhouse? We were given an option to purchase Patty's place, and we'll do it if you'll run it."

She didn't move. She could feel the smile on her face start to slip and tried to bolster it up. When she looked over at his family sitting there with her grandmother, she felt…she wasn't sure. But she knew that this wasn't what she wanted.

"I can't. I'm so sorry." She walked past him and toward her grandmother. It was all she could do not to break down and start screaming. "Grandmother, you are not a part of my life. I'm over eighteen and have no use for you. So I tell you this with all sincerity. Fuck off."

Chapter 20

Jesse watched his mother walk in. It had been two weeks since Joey had left the building, and today was moving day for him. He sat down in the chair that he was taking with him as soon as the movers showed up. And it couldn't be soon enough.

"Mom. If this is about the merger deal, then I finished the paperwork this morning. Royce just has to sign off on it." He knew that wasn't it. She'd been in here every day asking if he'd found Joey. He hadn't, and he didn't want to talk about it again.

"Good. He'll be happy. When are the movers coming?" She picked up a picture frame out of a box and put it back before she looked at him. "Jesse?"

"They're on their way. We should be finished up before the end of the day. Did you and Kasey get all the shopping finished?" He remembered vaguely that they were going for something for another thing, but he didn't remember the details.

"Yes. We saw Joey too." He didn't want to react, but his heart took a sudden skip, and he felt like he was going to pass out. "She's working, she said. I guess she's still living where she can, though. When Kasey asked her where she was staying, she said that she was still working on that."

He had to clear his throat twice before he could get the lump there to move. "Did she get her check from Doyle? He said he'd make sure she got it from the insurance company. That was really nice of them to give her a finder's fee, don't you think?"

He snapped his mouth closed. He didn't like babblers, and he wasn't going to do it now that she'd ripped his heart out and tossed it on the floor back to him. He reached down and touched the ring in his pocket. He'd not been able to put it back in the safe since Kylie had given it to him that day. She and Kasey were still mad at him and hadn't spoken to him since.

"I don't think so. If he did, she didn't mention it." She picked up another item off his desk and put it back. He had a feeling she wanted to say something to him but was sure he didn't want to hear it.

"Why are you here?" She turned to look at him with a raised brow. He took several deep breaths while he pulled his anger back to him like a shield. "You've been in here every day trying something to get me to tell you what happened. I don't know. She left me and told Doyle to tell me to stay away. I'm staying just like she said."

"What did you tell her that day?" He rolled his eyes and sat down when she asked. "You said you offered her a job, and she walked away. What did you say to her exactly?"

"I told her that we'd been able to purchase the greenhouse and that I needed to know if she'd run it." She sat down across from him as he continued. "She just looked at me then told her grandmother to fuck off and left. I don't know how many times—"

"Did you tell her that you loved her?" He nodded. "So when you offered her the job, did she know that you were hoping she'd take it as your wife and not an employee?"

"I'd already told her that we were getting married. She isn't that dense that she figured I was asking her to run the place as my live-in girlfriend." He stood up again and started taking things off the walls. "She left, and that's all I know. If you wanted more information, then you should have asked her."

"Take it down some, young man. You're still my son, and I will hurt you in ways you can't imagine."

He turned to look at her, his heart no longer able to just beat in his chest as if nothing had happened to it. "I don't think even you can hurt me any more than she did." She walked over and put her hands on his cheeks. "Mom, I love her so much."

The slap to his cheek hurt and stunned him. He took a step back when she looked like she was going to hit him again. Before he could ask her what the hell that was about, she poked him in the chest. "You *told* her she was marrying you. You *told* her that you loved her. You were awfully full of telling her what was what weren't you?" Before he could speak, she held up her hand. "You didn't ask her for her hand, did you? I would bet that you didn't even see if she loved you. Did she tell you that she loved you?"

"No, but—"

"She did Kasey and Kylie."

That shut him up. He looked at the door and wondered if they were in their offices. He was ready to find out when his mother spoke again.

199

"I don't believe she's ever said those words to anyone, do you? And I doubt very much anyone ever said them to her without making her feel like she should be grateful for the words."

"I never said them to her for that. I never…I never said them to her and had her believe me." He sat down hard on the couch. "I'm such an asshole."

His mom laughed. "Yes, you are. Especially if you keep sitting there when she's out there somewhere looking for something only you can give her."

He stood up and started for the door just as someone knocked. The fucking movers. He looked at his mom.

"Go, I got this. Find her and make her believe you."

He started for the elevator and went to his sister-in-law's office instead. They were laughing, and when he walked in, they stopped and glared. He couldn't take that anymore. Walking to both of them, he kissed them both on the cheeks and hugged them.

"Thank you." He looked at them when Kasey started cussing. "What did I do now?"

"She won the bet," Kasey said as she pointed at Kylie. "I said you'd be at least another week, she said today." She looked him in the face with narrow eyes. "You going after her, or do I have to beat your ass again?"

"Do you know where she is?" He wasn't going to point out she'd been able to kick his butt before because she'd been six months pregnant and he'd let her win. "I want to go and get her, and if you tell me where she is, then it will be that much quicker."

Ten minutes later, he was driving toward the empty buildings on Tenth Street and trying his best to think of what to say. He hadn't realized it was so late. And he was pretty sure a simple sorry wasn't going to cut it.

~~~

"I see." She didn't really see it at all but knew that arguing with the man wasn't going to get her any closer to a place to live. She told him goodbye and left the apartment complex.

This was the fifth complex that she'd been to today. There was something wrong with her application at the first place, and the second wouldn't take her because she wasn't thirty. She still didn't know why it mattered how old she was but had left when he threatened to have her arrested for trespassing. She went to the third place and was told that without a prior, verifiable address, he couldn't rent to her. She was pretty sure that her home now wouldn't be verifiable since she was living there without heat or electricity. She had running water, all cold and all she wanted, but no bill to show that she lived there.

This place had been the shortest visit yet. All she'd done was say she was here about the apartment.

"Rented it an hour ago," he'd said. She was too tired and too discouraged to point out that the "for rent" sign was still hanging and that the paper had said there were three for rent. She was going by the little shop near her home when she looked in the window.

The help wanted sign there looked accusatory to her. She'd been trying to get something that was more full-time, but...the four jobs she was working now were killing her, but she didn't need to sleep that much, did she? She walked in and asked for an application. She had it filled out and turned back in, in ten minutes. That was another thing; not having a phone made it difficult to have people call her back if she got the job.

After telling the girl behind the counter that she'd be back this way tomorrow, she left. It had started to snow again. Shivering in her coat, she wondered how she was going to stay warm this winter. Depressed more than she could almost handle, she tried to think of something else.

The owner wasn't in a lot when she applied for jobs and wondered just how they stayed in business when they never seemed to check up on things. She walked the rest of the way to her building with her head down and her heart heavy.

She missed the Hunters, and she missed Jesse a great deal. She missed his smile, his laugh, and especially the way he touched her. She knew that what he'd said to her that he loved her, wasn't true. Why on earth he would love someone like her was beyond comprehension. He was a fancy, rich lawyer while she was an uneducated, homeless person who couldn't find a job.

It was dark by the time she walked into the building she'd been staying in. She worked her way to the second floor, constantly looking for anyone or anything that might try to hurt her. She reached up and touched her jaw, where just this morning, someone had taken exception to her standing at the stop sign near him. People were just strange.

When she walked into her little office, she cried out when she saw someone standing in the window. Before she could back away, he spoke. Jesse Hunter was in her space.

"I was getting worried. I thought you'd be back before this late." He glanced out the window again before continuing. "It's coming down really hard now. We might have a foot by morning."

Nodding, she waited. A million questions popped into her

mind, and after she got answers to those, she was reasonably sure that many more would replace them. She looked around the office she'd been using for the past two weeks and saw that someone had brought in some more things.

"I don't want your charity. Whatever you brought, you can take with you when you leave. I don't know how you found—"

"It's mine. All of it, it's mine. I didn't know if you had enough to share, so I brought some things I thought I might need. I can get more as I see what you have." She didn't understand what he was talking about.

"You have to go. As I've said before, I don't want anything to do with—"

"I love you. Very much as a matter of fact." That shut her up. "And I can't, no that's not right, I don't want to live without you. I miss you in my bed and—"

"I'm sure there any number of women who would join you in your bed. You need to pack up your stuff and leave. Now. I'm not kidding." She watched as he moved slowly toward a box on the floor and started to unpack it. "What are you doing? I told you that you have to take it with you."

"I heard you. I'm not leaving you. I love you." He stood up again and started toward her. "I've been an ass. More, actually. I think we can add overbearing, dickhead, and prick. That one Kasey called me several times."

"If you think you're going to get an argument from me, then you'll be disappointed." He was still coming toward her slowly. "Stop right there. You still have your stuff to gather up."

He did stop when he was close enough for her to touch. And she wanted to. Badly. When he reached up and pulled her cap off, she was surprised at his smile. It was so sad.

"Do you love me, Joey? Even a little? I think you do, but I'm beginning to realize that I've not heard you say so. Not that I've given you a reason to love me, but I would still like to know." He ran his finger down her cheek, and she moaned at the feel. "I love the sounds you make when I touch you."

"You can't...the sex is—was good, but that doesn't make it lasting. I don't want to have someone only want me around because they are horny." She flushed at her words. "I'm not all that good at it anyway, contrary to what you've been told."

"I don't care what she said. Your grandmother can bite my ass for all I care. And maybe at first, we were having sex, but after I fell in love, that's what we were doing, making love." She snorted at him, and he smiled. "Would you like me to show you the difference between sex and making love? I'm up for it if you are."

His brows wiggled, and she laughed. "You know what I am, Jesse. I'm a woman who has no—"

"Don't send me away, Joey. Please? I can't live without you. I want you to..." He dropped to his knee and took her hand into his. "I would like it very much if you would marry me. I would very much love it if you'd come home with me and have children with me. I want to spend the rest of my life loving you, showing you how much I love you. I need you in my life."

She wiped at the tears she couldn't control. She looked around the office and then back at him. "You were going to live here with me."

"Yes. For however long it took for you to believe me that I love you." He glanced around the room then back up at her. "I don't suppose there's a coffee machine hidden amongst your things, is there?"

Laughing, she answered. "No. Not even hot water for a shower. You might want to reconsider your living arrangements."

He kissed her hand. "Have you? I'm not leaving here without you. And you still haven't told me if you love me or not." He shifted on his knees. "I love you, baby."

She thought about telling him no, she didn't love him, but she couldn't. She looked around the office again and didn't look at him. What she had to say was going to be hard enough without seeing his face. "I dated this person when I was in high school. I knew that he was going with someone, but I didn't know he was married. I was a sophomore, and he a senior. His wife had had to drop out of school the year before I started there because she was pregnant. We dated for a while before I…before he…"

"Did he force you, Joey?" She backed away from the anger in his voice as he stood up, and she hit the wall behind her. He moved to her slowly as he spoke. "I'm going to have to kill him, you know that, don't you? No one hurts the woman I love and gets by with it." His smile was scary, and she was pretty sure he was serious.

"He's dead. She, his wife, killed him." When she tried to look away again, he held her chin and told her to tell him. "She found out. Not about me, though I don't know why she didn't. We never tried to be…I didn't know there was a reason to be discreet about it. There were others. Four of them, as a matter of fact, and two of them were pregnant. I'd made him use a condom the one and only time." She took a deep breath. "He didn't force me. I was willing, though it wasn't all that good. He said it was me and…well, I believed him."

"Did she hurt any of the other women?"

Joey shook her head.

"Tell me, love. It's eating at you, and you need to get rid of this."

"He was with some friends of his. I'd told him the week before that I no longer wanted to see him. He said it was fine by him. I was a lousy lay anyway. She came up in their car with their baby in the front seat. She simply got out of the car, left the door open, and fired at him. The first shot hit him in the groin. The second in his head. He was dead before he hit the ground. Then she turned the gun on herself and killed herself."

"Christ. You were there, weren't you?"

It wasn't really a question, but she answered it with a nod. "I was working at the ice cream parlor. I was at the window when they...Derick was...had been telling them what he and I had been up to. I...I thought for sure she was going to kill me too. But she...the baby sat there playing with her toys as if her entire life hadn't just changed."

She was sobbing now, and when he pulled her to him, she let him. He held her, ran his fingers down her back, and kissed her head. He was speaking, saying things she really didn't understand, but she was comforted by it. When she felt him pick her up, she wrapped her arms around him and let him carry her from the building and to his car.

Neither of them spoke as he drove. She wasn't surprised when they drove up his driveway. When he came around the car to help her out, she stopped him with a hand to his chest. It was past time. "I love you. I think I always have. But I'm not—"

"Yes, you are. You're going to marry me as soon as I can

get the arrangements made." He kissed her quickly on the mouth. "We, my dear, have not been using protection, and I hope like hell you're already pregnant with our child." With a loud shout of joy, he picked her up again and took her in the house. Samuel and Lowell met them in the hall with surprised looks. "She is marrying me, and I'm going to go up and make love to her all night. Don't bother us unless the house is on fire." He set her down and reached into his pocket. "Here. If it rings, tell them…tell them I'm in love and can't come to the phone right now."

With that, he picked her up and took her up the stairs three at a time.

Chapter 21

Annamarie put the phone back in the cradle with a smile. She looked at the people in the office with her and grinned bigger. "He's not coming in."

"What is that supposed to mean? He said he'd be here and…he'd better be on his death bed is all I can say for him." Royce ran his hand through his hair for the umpteenth time. "I swear he's getting his as…butt kicked for this."

"He's in love. And Samuel said that he told them not to disturb them unless the house was on fire. Samuel said that the young miss looked to be in the same frame of mind." That stopped Royce in mid-step. "I think he's getting just what he needs."

"He didn't force her, did he?"

Annamarie smiled at Kasey, who she knew told Jesse where to find Joey.

"I would really hate to have to castrate him if he did."

Daniel, ever practical, spoke. "Well, we can do this without him. As you guys know, this is my last day here, too, but I'm still our lawyer in personal things. Doyle here is going to run the security department with Kasey's help until he has it the way he wants." After a few more questions from their newest employee, Doyle, they got down to other business. Namely, the Jennings issue. "There are nine buildings in the district where we were looking. The real-estate agency that she worked for is willing to let us purchase them cheap." Curtis handed them all a folder. "I didn't say we'd take them yet. I think if we let him stew a bit longer, he'll come down more."

"Purchase them all and don't haggle. This wasn't his fault and tell him that we will use him for future projects if we need anything." Royce closed the file. "I don't want us to look like we're doing something underhanded because his employee was a crook."

"What are we going to do with nine buildings? I mean, there is a reason they were all empty. The economy sucks right now." Daniel got up to pace. "I know you want to take advantage of the deal, but nine?"

"I want to use two of them." Kylie spoke up then flushed. "I have an idea to use two of them if it's okay. I would like to change them to studios for upcoming artists. A place they can go and work. All media too."

"I like that. Free of charge too. And we can see if we can get the colleges to give credit to them." Kasey laughed. "Heck, I might even give a try at one of them."

And they were off and running. An hour later, they had the workings of two studios that would not only give new artists a place to work, but a gallery to show their work in. In exchange for the usage, they would have to work for the complex in some capacity until they left. Annamarie thought that it was brilliant.

"I think there is another project we can get going too. This is something that Jared and I have often thought of. A place to get construction experience for kids in high school." Curtis leaned back as he continued. "The buildings are going to need some work anyway, and the labor would be spotty at best, but it would be a way to put a bunch of men to work training and working with kids."

By lunchtime, they had it covered. Oh, she knew there were going to be issues. What project didn't have them? But she loved her kids all the more for what they were willing to put back into the community. Now all she had to do was get Daniel married off.

Annamarie smiled. Daniel glared at her, and she knew just what he was thinking. He was next. Well, he was, and he was going to be the most fun of them all.

She didn't know who she was or what kind of help she could bring him, but she was sure it was going to be a blast. She watched the other two women in her son's lives and smiled. Kasey and Kylie, and now Joey, were going to make her a grandmother so many times she was going to need a bigger rocker to rock them all in.

~~~

Jesse reached blindly for the woman in his bed. He had brought her back here last night and showed her the difference between sex and making love and had worn them both out. But all he got now was cold sheets. Opening one eye, he looked around and saw that her side of the bed was empty. He reached for his cell phone to call Samuel and remembered that he'd given it to Samuel. Smiling, he got up. If she was gone again, he was going to enjoy beating her lovely ass. He was just pulling on his pants when she came out of the bathroom.

"I took a bath." She flushed and tightened his robe around

her. "I was kind of sore, and I took a bath."

"Did I hurt you?" He looked in her face when she stared at him. He saw panic and terror and something he wasn't sure of. "Joey, did I hurt you?"

"No. Not at all. I enjoyed…I was just sore, that's all." She didn't move, so he went to her. "I thought a bath would feel good after the tumble I took before you got there."

She'd told him about the fall. Someone had hit her too, but she told him that she was all right. He saw the bruise on her cheek; it was just starting to turn. Jesse ran his finger down the coloring and lifted her chin up. "So if I said to you, let's go back to bed; it would be too painful for you, and you'd tell me no, right?"

"No," she nearly screamed at him. She continued in a much quieter voice. "No. That would be fine with me. If that's what you want. I enjoyed last night. A lot. Did you?"

He brushed his mouth over hers slowly, touching but not tasting her. When she sighed against his mouth, he felt the heat of it scorch his skin. He pulled her closer to him and wrapped his hands around her waist.

"I'd very much like to make love to you again. I was actually thinking that I'd do it in the shower, but since you've already had a bath, I guess that's not going to — "

"I could use a shower. I just soaked in the tub, so I really didn't get clean." She took a step back, then another. He watched as she toyed with the belt. "If you'd like for me to, I could wash your back for you."

She untied the belt and then let it fall to the floor. He watched mesmerized as she opened the front slowly, running her fingers up and down her skin from her navel to her neck. His cock surged to life, and he growled at her.

"You're playing with fire, Joey. I mean it, you keep playing like that and I'll... mother fuck."

The robe opened and she let it hang onto her shoulders for a few seconds before it too fell to the floor. When she stood before him naked, he watched as she used her hands to lift her breasts, tweak her nipples, before she let her head fall back on a moan.

"I'm not playing, Jesse. Not at all." She raised her head and looked at him through hooded eyes. "Nor am I a slow learner. I want to play with you. Will you let me?"

His strangled "yes" spilled from his lips before he could stop it. He was pretty sure she hadn't planned on anything but an affirmative answer, but he had thought to be the teacher, not the pupil in their lovemaking. She was advancing much faster than he'd thought. He decided to enjoy every second of her.

"Come here then. I want to give you a bath." He followed her into the bathroom and noticed the candles burning on every surface. There was water in the tub and, with it, flower blossoms and rose petals. There were two towels hanging on the warmer as well.

"You didn't take a bath, did you?"

She shook her head.

"And you were coming out to get me when I got up."

This time, she nodded and touched him.

"You said that I could enjoy myself. I thought you meant you included. Did you?" She ran her fingers over his nipples, then leaned in and nipped at the left then the right before looking up at him. "I can stop if you want me to."

"You are going to pay for this, I hope you know." She ran her fingers along the waistband of his pants, and he was very glad he'd opted for lounge pants and not jeans this morning.

"I certainly hope so. Let me help you undress." She had his pants off in record time. Every time he reached for her, she'd step back. "No, this is for you this time. When you touch me, I can't think. I want to take you there for a change."

"Say it to me again. Tell me, and I'm all yours." He clenched his teeth together when she brushed her hair against his cock when she dropped down to take his pants the rest of the way off. "Joey?"

"I love you, Jesse Hunter, and will marry you as soon as you can arrange it." He nearly fell over when she licked his cock from tip to root. He grabbed the counter and tried to stay upright while she sucked him into her mouth.

"Christ." He wanted to wrap his hand into her hair and help her let him fuck her, but he was afraid. If he touched her, would she quit, or would she finish him off by not quitting? "Joey, please, let me fuck you."

She looked up at him, his cock glistening with her salvia, and winked. He wasn't sure what that meant, but he was pretty sure she wasn't going to let him do what he needed.

When she pulled away and leaned back on her heels, he tried to catch his breath. But she wasn't finished with him just yet. When she stood up and leaned over the counter, her ass presented to him, he nearly swallowed his tongue.

"You can fuck me, but don't come. And when I say to stop, you have to stop." She looked at him through the mirror. "If you don't stop or come before I say so, then I won't ever do this again. Okay?"

"Yes. I'll behave." Or he'd behave as well as he could. Walking up behind her, he marveled at how she fit him. Her pussy was right there for him, his cock ready to enter her.

Slowly, he moved into her sheath, pulling out a little with every move forward. He felt the sweat run down his spine and had a thought that his plan to drive her over the edge quickly was backfiring. He gripped her hips and pulled her back to him as he surged forward. He looked at her in the reflection.

She was beautiful. Her nipples were hard and long, and every time he moved into her or out, they would sway in time to his thrusts. She bit her lip, worried it as he quickened his pace, her eyes dark with lust. When she screamed out his name, tightened around his cock, he watched as she came, her climax rushing over her entire body. He could feel his own balls tighten to his body, felt the warm rush of his own climax coming when she told him to stop.

He stopped. He was sure if either of them moved right now, he'd come, but for now, he was stopped. When she stood and pulled away from him and his cock, he whimpered. He was on the point of begging when she turned, dropped to her knees, and took him into her mouth. He couldn't think, couldn't do anything but wait for her to give him permission. When it came, her release on him, his cock let go, and he filled her throat.

Over and over, he fucked her luscious mouth. His climax seemed to go on forever, then she reached between his legs and cupped his balls, bringing another climax hard from him.

When he finished, his body drained, he fell back against the counter and held on. If she touched him again right now, he would die. He wasn't kidding himself either. She'd nearly done so already.

Taking his hand, she led him to the tub. The water was warm, almost hot when he stepped in, and he watched as she entered behind him. When she asked him to sit, she moved to in front of him and into his lap. Neither of them said anything for a long while.

He reached for the large sponge on the edge of the tub and filled it with soap. He'd have to have her get something that didn't smell like him soon. Or maybe not. He liked the thought of her carrying his scent. When he lifted her arm to wash her, she started talking.

"I want you to know that if you think I need you to marry me, I don't. I mean, I love you, but you don't have to feel you have to marry me."

He washed her other arm; then she lifted her leg. He wanted to run his tongue down its length to her center, but his body wasn't having it. She'd drained him.

"I have to marry you, and that's final. I have plans that you have to help me with." He put more soap on the sponge as he washed her other leg. "I want to be in politics soon. That is one of the reasons I went out on my own. First, to see if I could do it, secondly, to see if I could succeed at being on my own."

She turned slightly. "Won't my background hurt your chances of being president? I mean, I don't exactly have a stellar background."

"I didn't say president. I said politics. There's a big difference between the two. I was thinking more of being the state representative."

She turned all the way this time and stared at him with a furrow in her brow. He couldn't imagine what was going through her head but figured she'd tell him soon enough. When she did, he nearly laughed.

"And what's wrong with you being president? Nothing.

You don't aim for the middle ring when the top one is open to you. You have just as much right to be the big guy as I do your missus big guy." She turned around and took the sponge from him. "Besides, what would my grandmother say if my husband didn't try very hard? She'd tell you that I slowed you down. And our children? What would they think of their daddy if he settled? No, you're going to go for the White House or nothing at all."

Jesse laughed. His entire body was relaxed, sated, and happy. He pulled her around to him and kissed her on the mouth. He adjusted her so that she was straddled across his lap and pulled her to him. "I love you, Joey Foster. I love you with all my being and will be honored if you would allow me to make you missus big guy."

"Well, of course, you will. How silly would that be if I wasn't? You need someone to bathe you."

They spent the entire day together. Samuel pampered his friend Lowell, and the other man seemed to bask in it. Lowell promised to show her how to cook some easy things, and she promised to show him how to fight. The phone rang at around four, and he answered it with a light heart.

"I was wondering if you and Joey could come over for dinner. We've been making plans, and I'd like to get you up to par before we move completely out. The family is going to need your help on a few things. Are you up for it?" Jesse watched Joey try to toss hash browns in the air and catch them in a skillet before he answered his brother Daniel.

"Why don't you all come here? Joey is learning to cook, and Samuel was just saying that we've never entertained here. I have an announcement to make." He smiled when his brother was quiet. "Have I rendered you speechless?"

"You're going to do it, aren't you? You're going to run for state representative, aren't you? Hot damn, I knew it. I can't tell you how happy —"

"That's not all of it. Joey has her heart set on the White House. I can't disappoint her. She wants to pick out a dinnerware pattern." His brother was no longer quiet but laughing. Jesse wasn't sure if he should be offended or not and nearly asked him what the fuck was so funny.

"We'll be there. All of us, even if I have to tie them up and bring them. And I want to make this announcement if you don't mind. You tell them you're going to get married and I tell them I'm going to be your campaign manager. Holy hell, I'm going to get laid because of this."

They hung up a few minutes later, and he told his cook to expect them for dinner. He pulled his future wife into his arms and simply held her. Life was just about to get very interesting. And he couldn't wait.

About the Author

Kathi Barton, the author of the bestselling series Force of Nature, lives in Nashport, Ohio, with her husband, Paul. In addition to writing full-time, Kathi likes to spend time with her eight grandkids, three children, and three children-in-law. She writes to relax and have fun.

Her muse, a cross between Jimmy Stewart and Hugh Jackman, brings them to life for her readers in a way that has them coming back time and again for more. Her favorite genre is paranormal romance, with a great deal of spice. You can visit Kathi on line and drop her an email if you'd like. She loves hearing from her fans. aaronskiss@gmail.com.

Follow Kathi on her blog: http://kathisbartonauthor.blogspot.com/

www.ingramcontent.com/pod-product-compliance
Lightning Source LLC
Chambersburg PA
CBHW032120170626
46808CB00006B/2024